GET CARTER

The original novel of the classic cult film...

Doncaster, and Jack Carter is home for a funeral – his brother Frank's. Frank's car was found at the bottom of a cliff, with Frank inside. He was not only dead drunk but dead as well. Jack thinks his death doesn't add up, so he decides to talk to a few people after the funeral. He does, but is soon told to stop. By Gerald and Les. They run a London porn 'firm' and Jack's their hit man. Now Frank was a mild man and did as he was told, but Jack's not a bit like that .

Please note: *This book contains material which may not be suitable to all our readers.*

GET CARTER

GET CARTER

by

Ted Lewis

Dales Large Print Books
Long Preston, North Yorkshire,
BD23 4ND, England.

British Library Cataloguing in Publication Data.

Lewis, Ted
   Get Carter.

   A catalogue record of this book is
   available from the British Library

   ISBN   1-84262-124-6 pbk

First published in Great Britain as *Get Carter* in 1992
by Allison & Busby
an imprint of Virgin Publishing

First published in Great Britain as *Jack's Return Home* in 1970
by Michael Joseph Ltd.

Published in Large Print 2001 by arrangement with
Allison & Busby Ltd.

Dales Large Print is an imprint of Library Magna Books Ltd.

Printed and bound in Great Britain by
T.J. (International) Ltd., Cornwall, PL28 8RW

Thursday

The rain rained.

It hadn't stopped since Euston. Inside the train it was close, the kind of closeness that makes your fingernails dirty even when all you're doing is sitting there looking out of the blurring windows. Watching the dirty backs of houses scudding along under the half-light clouds. Just sitting and looking and not even fidgeting.

I was the only one in the compartment. My slip-ons were off. My feet were up. *Penthouse* was dead. I'd killed the *Standard* twice. I had three nails left. Doncaster was forty minutes off.

I looked along the black mohair to my socks. I flexed a toe. The toenail made a sharp ridge in the wool. I'd have to cut them when I got in. I might be doing a lot of footwork over the weekend.

I wondered if I'd have time to get some fags from the buffet at Doncaster before my connection left.

If it was open at five-to-five on a Thursday afternoon in mid-October.

I lit up anyway.

It was funny that Frank never smoked.

7

Most barmen do. In between doing things. Even one drag to make it seem as if they're having a break. But Frank never touched them. Not even a Woody just to see what it was like when we were kids down Jackson Street. He'd never wanted to know.

He didn't drink scotch either.

I picked up the flask from off the *Standard* and unscrewed the cap and took a pull. The train rocked and a bit of scotch went on my shirt, a biggish spot, just below the collar.

But not as much as had been down the front of the shirt Frank had been wearing when they'd found him. Not nearly so much.

They hadn't even bothered to be careful; they hadn't even bothered to be clever.

I screwed the cap on and put the flask back on the seat. Beyond fast rain and dark low clouds thin light appeared for a second as the hurrying sun skirted the rim of a hill. The erratic beam caught the silver flask and illuminated the engraved inscription.

It said: 'From Gerald and Les to Jack. With much affection on his thirty-eighth birthday.'

Gerald and Les were the blokes I worked for. They looked after me very well because that's what I did for them. They were in the property business. Investment. Speculation. That kind of thing. You know.

Pity it had to finish. But sooner or later

8

Gerald'd find out about me and Audrey. And when that happened I'd rather be out of the way. Working for Stein. In the sun. With Audrey getting brown all over. And no rain.

Doncaster Station. Gloomy wide windy areas of rails and platforms overhung with concrete and faint neon. Rain noiselessly emphasising the emptiness. The roller front of W.H. Smith's pulled hard down.

I walked along the enclosed overhead corridor that led to the platform where my connection was waiting. There was nobody else in the corridor. The echoes of my footsteps raced before me. I turned left at a sign that said Platform Four and walked down the steps. The diesel was humming and ready for off. I got in, slammed the door and sat down in a three-seater. I put my hold-all down on the seat, stood up, took off my green suède overcoat and draped it over the hold-all.

I looked down the carriage. There was about a dozen passengers all with their backs to me. I turned round and looked through into the guard's van. The guard was reading the paper. I took my flask out and had a quick one. I put the flask back in the hold-all and felt for my fags. But I'd already smoked the last one.

At first there's just the blackness. The rocking of the train, the reflections against the raindrops and the blackness. But if you keep looking beyond the reflections you eventually notice the glow creeping into the sky.

At first it's slight and you think maybe a haystack or a petrol tanker or something is on fire somewhere over a hill and out of sight. But then you notice that the clouds themselves are reflecting the glow and you know that it must be something bigger. And a little later the train passes through a cutting and curves away towards the town, a small bright concentrated area of light and beyond and around the town you can see the causes of the glow, the half dozen steelworks stretching to the rim of the semicircular bowl of hills, flames shooting upwards – soft reds pulsing on the insides of melting shops, white heat sparking in blast furnaces – the structures of the works black against the collective glow, all of it looking like a Disney version of the Dawn of Creation. Even when the train enters the short sprawl of backyards and behinds of petrol stations and rows of too-bright street lights, the reflected ribbon of flame still draws your attention up into the sky.

I handed in my ticket and walked through the barrier to the front of the station where the car park was. A few of my fellow passengers got into cars, the rest made for the waiting double-decker bus. Rain drifted idly across the shiny concrete. I looked round for a taxi. Nothing. There was a phone box near the booking office so I got in it, found 'Taxis' in the directory and phoned one. They said five minutes. I put the phone down and decided I'd rather have the rain than the smell of old cigarette ends.

Outside I stood and stared across the car park. The bus and the cars had gone. Directly opposite me was the entrance to the car park and beyond that was the road with its loveless lights and its council houses. It all looked as it had looked eight years ago when I'd seen it last. A good place to say goodbye to.

I remembered what Frank had said to me at dad's funeral, the last time I'd seen the place.

I'd been eating an egg sandwich and talking to Mrs Gorton when Frank had limped over and asked me to pop upstairs with him for a minute.

I'd followed him into our old bedroom and he'd taken a letter and he'd said to me, 'Read it.' I'd said, 'Who's it from?' He'd said, 'Read it.' Still eating the sandwich, I'd looked at the postmark. It had come from Sunderland. The date was four days earlier. I'd taken the letter out of the envelope and

11

I'd flicked it over and looked at the signature.

When I'd seen who it was from, I'd looked at Frank.

'Read it,' he'd said.

The cab swung into the car park. It was a modern car with a lit-up sign in the middle of its roof. It stopped in front of me and the driver got out and walked round and opened the passenger door.

'Mr Carter?'

I walked towards the car and he took my hold-all and put it on the back seat.

'Lovely weather,' he said.

I got in and he got in.

'Where was it?' he said. 'The George?'

'That's right,' I said.

The car began to move. I felt in my pocket and pulled out my packet of fags but I forgot it was empty. The driver pulled a packet of Weights out of his pocket.

'Here,' he said, 'have one of these.'

'Thanks,' I said. I lit us both up.

'Staying long, are you?' he asked.

'Depends.'

'On business?'

'Not really.'

He drove on a bit more.

'Know it round here, do you?'

'A bit.'

We were driving along the same road we'd been on since the car park. The lights were getting brighter. In front of us was the main street.

It was a strange place. Too big for a town, too small for a city. As a kid it had always struck me that it was like some western boom town. There was just the main street where there was everything you needed and everything else just dribbled off towards the ragged edges of the town. Council houses started immediately behind Woolworth's. Victorian terraces butted up to the side of Marks and Spencer's. The gasworks over-shadowed the Kardomah. The swimming baths and the football ground faced each other only yards away from the corporation allotments.

And really it was a boom town. Thirty years ago it had been just another village hiding in the lee of the Wolds. Then they'd found the sandstone. Thirty years later what had been a small village was a big town and would have been bigger if it hadn't been for the ring of steelworks hemming in the sprawl.

On the surface it was a dead town. The kind of place not to be in on a Sunday afternoon. But it had its levels. Choose a level, present the right credentials and the town was just as good as anywhere else. Or as bad.

And there was money. And it was spread all over because of the steelworks. Council

13

houses with a father and a mother and a son and a daughter all working. Maybe eighty quid a week coming in. A good place to operate if you were a governor who owned a lot of small time set-ups. The small time stuff took the money from the council houses. And there were a lot of council houses. Once I'd scrawled for a betting shop on Priory Hill. Christ, I'd thought, when I'd happened to find out how much they took in a week. Give me a string of those places and you could keep Chelsea. And Kensington. If the overheads were anything like related to what that tight bastard I'd been working for had been paying me.

We pulled up outside 'The George'. It said 'The George Hotel', but all it was was a big boozer that did bed and breakfast. It was all Snowcemed and the woodwork was painted blue and the windows were fake lattice but I knew inside it was crummy. When I first started going in pubs when I was fifteen, 'The George' was the one boozer I daren't try. It looked so respectable on the outside. Later I learned different. I still didn't go in, but for different reasons. But at this moment it suited all right.

The driver whipped round the front of the car and opened my door. I got out. He opened the back door and got the hold-all.

'How much is that?' I said.

'Five bob,' he said.

'Here you are,' I said. I gave him seven and six.

'Thanks, mate,' he said. 'All the best.'

He made to take my bag towards the hotel.

'That's all right,' I said. 'I can manage.'

He gave me the bag. I began to turn away.

'Er,' he said, 'er, if you're off to be about during next few days and you need owt, driving anywhere, like, give us a ring. Right?'

I turned to look at him. The blue of the neon and the dead yellow of the high street light made him look as though he needed an oxygen tent. There was an earnest helpful look on his face. Rain looked like sweat on his forehead. I kept looking at him. The earnest helpful look changed.

'I told you,' I said. 'I can manage.'

He looked at the hold-all then at me, tracing back my words. He tried to frown, but the little bit of fear made him look more hurt than angry.

'I was only being helpful,' he said.

I smiled at him.

'Goodnight,' I said, and turned away.

I walked towards the door marked 'Saloon' and opened it. I didn't hear him close his.

Amateurs, I thought. Bloody stinking amateurs. I closed the door behind me.

15

You had to give the landlord credit. He'd really tried to make it look the kind of place that married couples in their forties would like to come to for the last hour on a Saturday night.

There was that heavy wallpaper in panels, the relief stuff that tried to look as though it was velvet. There was a photo-mural of Capri. There were wall seats in leatherette that looked as though they'd been put in a couple of years ago. There was formica on all the tabletops and also on top of the bar. There was some plastic wrought iron creating a pointless division. There was also a clean shirt on the landlord.

There were a couple of yobbo's playing a disc-only fruit machine. There was an old dad with a half-a-bitter and the *Racing Green,* and sitting next to him there was a very old brass in a trouser suit leaving her lipstick all over a glass of Guinness. But no sign at all of the person I was looking for.

It was quarter past seven.

I walked over to the bar. The landlord was looking at something in the till and thinking. The barman was leaning against the mirror at the back of the bar. He had his arms folded. His hairstyle was Irish Tony Curtis. Farther down the bar was a man of about thirty in a Marks & Spencer cardigan with a lovat green shirt open at the neck. He was sitting on a stool and looking at

16

himself in the mirror.

I put my hold-all down and looked at the barman. He didn't move.

'Pint of bitter,' I said.

He let his arms unfold, reached out for a pint mug and made his weary way to the pumps and without putting anything more into it than it needed he began to pull the pint.

'In a thin glass please,' I said.

The barman looked at me and the bloke down the bar looked at the barman.

'Why didn't you bloody well say?' said the barman, slowly putting the brakes on the beer.

'I was going to, but you were too fast for me.'

The bloke down the bar threw back his head and gave a short hard laugh.

The barman looked at the bloke and then looked back at me. The movement took him about thirty seconds. It took him another thirty seconds to decide not to call me a clever sod. Instead he found a thin glass and poured what was in the mug into it and topped it up from the pumps. After another fascinating minute the drink was in front of me.

'How much?' I said.

'One and ten,' said the barman.

I gave him one and ten and went and sat down on one of the leatherette seats as far

17

away from everybody else as possible. I took a long drink and settled down to wait. I was expecting her any minute.

Quarter of an hour passed and I got up and went over to the bar and got Speedy to pull me another pint. I walked over to my seat again, and out of sight, up a flight of stairs, a phone began to ring. The landlord stopped looking at what was or was not in the till and came round the bar and went up the stairs. I sat down and took a sip of my pint and the landlord reappeared at the foot of the stairs.

'Is there a Mr Carter in the bar?' he said, looking straight at me with that expression all publicans have when they answer the phone for somebody else.

I stood up.

'That's me,' I said.

He walked back to the bar without bothering to go into any further details. I walked over to the foot of the stairs and followed the distant sounds of the *Coronation Street* music until I arrived on the landing where the receiver was dangling from the pay phone. I picked it up.

'Hallo?' I said.

'Jack Carter?' she said.

'You were supposed to be here quarter of an hour ago.'

'I know. I can't come.'

'Why not?'

'Me husband. He's changed shifts. Ten to two.'

I didn't say anything.

'I've made all the arrangements,' she said.

'What time?'

'Half-past nine.'

'Did you get the flowers?'

'Yes.'

I took out a cigarette.

'Is Doreen at the house?'

'No. She's staying with a friend.'

'Who's with him then?'

'I don't know.'

'He's not on his own, is he?'

'I don't know.'

'Well you'd better go round and find out then.'

'I can't.'

'Why not?'

'Same reason as I couldn't meet you.'

Silence.

'Look,' I said, 'when can I see you?'

'You can't.'

'Will you be there tomorrow?'

'No.'

'Now look...'

'Door's on the latch,' she said. 'He's in front room.'

She rang off. I looked at the dead receiver for a few seconds, then put it back on the hook and went down the stairs and finished my pint standing up. Then I picked up my hold-all and went out into the rain.

I walked away from 'The George', turning left down a dark street of terraced houses with narrow front gardens. Above the rain and the blackness low clouds touched with pink from the steelworks sidled across the sky. I turned left again into another street exactly the same as the first except that at the end of it was a stretch of narrow road that ran out of the town between the steel works and up into the Wolds. I walked to the end of the street and opposite me on the other side of the exit road was Parker's Garage And Car Hire.

I crossed the road and tapped on the office door. Nobody was in sight. I tapped again, harder. A door beyond the filing cabinet opened. A man in overalls and a woollen hat with a bobble on top appeared. He crossed the office and opened the door.

He looked into my face and waited for me to tell him what I wanted.

'I'd like to hire a car,' I said.

'How long for?' he said.

'Only for a few days,' I said. 'I shan't be staying long.'

I drove up through the town but via the back routes that paralleled the High Street until I came to Holden Street, a street in which I knew every other house did Bed and

Breakfast; after Frank had been buried I didn't want to operate from the house, not with Doreen around. I didn't want her involved unless I could help it. I found one with a garage and parked the car in front of the house, walked up the path and knocked on the door and waited.

The house had gabled windows and a mean little porch. The top half of the front door was panelled in opaque glass with a border of little squares of coloured glass running along the top and the two sides. On either side of the door there were two more panels exactly the same except that they were narrower. Inside the hall a shadow approached the front door and opened it.

She wasn't bad. About forty, probably the right side of it, hair permed, squarish face, well powdered, big tits, open-necked blouse shoved tight into her skirt. No nonsense with the wrong people but what about the right ones?

She looked as though she might be pleased to see me.

'Am I in luck?' I said.

'What for?' she said.

'A room. Have you any vacant?'

'We have.'

'Oh, good,' I said. She stepped back to let me in. I hesitated.

'Look,' I said, 'the point is, I don't actually need one right now, tonight that is, it'll be tomorrow and Saturday, maybe Sunday.'

She altered her stance, resting all her weight on one leg.

'Oh, yes?' she said.

'Yes, you see. I'm staying with a friend for tonight, but you know how it is, it won't be convenient tomorrow, you know.'

'Her husband changes shifts tomorrow, does he?'

'Well, er, it's not exactly like that,' I said.

'No,' she said, beginning to turn away, 'it never is.'

'There's one other thing,' I said.

She turned back and adopted the stance again.

'See, I've got a car, and I know it'd be all right if I left it in the road, but I notice you've got a garage and I was wondering if it was empty if maybe I could put it in there. Tonight, like.'

She carried on looking at me.

'I mean,' I said, 'I'll pay.'

She looked at me a bit longer.

'Well, you can hardly park it outside her house, can you?' she said.

'Thanks,' I said, following her in, 'that's very nice of you, it really is.'

'I know,' she said.

She began to go up the stairs. Her legs were all right, and so was her bum, muscular but not as big as it would have been if she didn't look after herself. When she got to the top of the stairs she turned round while I was still watching her.

'Traveller are you?' she said.

'You could say that,' I said.

'I see,' she said.

She crossed a landing and opened a door. 'Will this do?' she said.

'Oh yes,' I said. 'Just the job.' I looked all round to show her how much I appreciated it. 'Just the job.' I took my wallet out. 'Look, I'll pay now and if you like I'll pay for to-night just to keep the room open.'

'That'd be a bloody silly thing to do,' she said. 'You're first one since Monday.'

'Oh, well, if you're sure,' I said. 'How much?'

'Fifty bob for two nights. Bed and breakfast. A pound'll do for garage. Let us know Sunday morning if you're staying.'

I took out the money and gave it to her. She folded it up and pushed it in her skirt pocket. It was a tight fit.

'And as I say,' I said, 'I'll pop round tomorrow tea-time and move it then if that's all right.'

'Whenever you like.'

'Good,' I said.

We walked down the stairs. At the door she said:

'I'll open the garage for you.'

I got in the car, reversed it and drove it up the bit of drive and sat there. She pushed up the sliding door. I drove in and got out.

'Look,' I said, 'will you be in all day tomorrow?'

'Why?'

'Well, I might need the car tomorrow afternoon and I'd like to collect it if you'll be here.'

'I'll be here all day after twelve,' she said.

'Oh, good,' I said. 'Fine.'

I walked out of the garage. I turned to face her.

'And thanks again.'

She just stared at me with no expression on her face although there was something there way back that might have been a smile, although if she'd have allowed it to surface it would have been a sarcastic one at that. She stopped staring and began to close the garage door.

I walked down the drive and on to the pavement and turned in the direction of the High Street. I smiled. It amused me, the picture she'd got of me, the way she thought she'd got me weighed up. It might turn out to be helpful.

As I got closer to the High Street I noticed it wasn't raining any more.

I turned left and walked up the High Street. I passed the Oxford Cinema and Eastoes Remnants and Walton's sweetshop. When we were lads Walton's doorway was where we always used to stand and watch

24

the world go by. It was the best doorway in the High Street. Big enough to accommodate about twelve lads and in winter it was the least draughty. Pecker Wood, Arthur Coleman, Piggy Jacklin, Nezzer Eyres, Ted Rose, Alan Stamp. We all used to congregate there before the pictures and if we didn't have the money for the pictures we'd stand there until it was time for us to go home. Jack Coleman, Howard Shepherdson, Dave Patchett. I wondered what had happened to them all

And of course Frank. But I knew what had happened to him.

And that was something I was going to put right.

Now I was at Jackson Street. On the corner where Rowson's Grocers used to be was the same shop with the same thirties front but it had been painted yellow (the woodwork, the window frame) and instead of Rowson's Family Grocer on the fascia it said Hurdy Gurdy in Barnum and Bailey lettering and behind the glass instead of Dandelion and Burdock bottles on faded yellow crêpe paper and instead of Player's Airmen showcards and Vimto signs there were poove clothes and military uniforms and blow-ups of groups. The shop butted up against the row of villa-type bay windowed houses that ran down one side of Jackson Street and up the other. At the end of the

25

street a long way away was an iron railing fence and beyond that there used to be the waste ground, the browny yellow grass that led you to the drain, the narrow soggy dyke where Frank and I and others would go up and drop down out of sight of the villas and do anything we wanted to do. At least, I used to, and some of the others, but when Valerie Marshbanks showed everybody her knickers and charged a penny a wank, in the bushes, one at a time with Christine Hall who liked to watch, Frank would never be there, but he'd know what was going on, and when I'd get home, he'd be reading his comic, and he wouldn't say anything to me, he'd just make me feel fucking awful, and very often he'd keep it up so long that Mam would tell him to straighten his bloody face up else get to bed and he'd just pick up his comic and go up, not looking at me. And when I'd go up, the light would be off, and I'd know he was awake, and that would be worse, having to get in bed in the dark listening to him thinking. I wouldn't be able to get to sleep for ages because he'd be there awake and I'd be awake because I hardly dared breathe knowing he was thinking about me.

I walked along Jackson Street. Now at the end the railings were still there and some of the grass, but the dyke wasn't, it had been filled in and there was a small light engineering works, yellow brick under the street light with a lathe on overtime inside.

I got to number forty-eight. The curtains were drawn, of course, but there was a light on in the hall illuminating the frosted glass panels and the privet hedge four feet away from the bay windows.

I opened the front door.

There was new wallpaper on the wall, contemporary, with lobster pots and fishermen's nets and grounded single masted-yachts, all light browns and pale greens. He'd hardboarded the banisters in, and painted the hardboard and put pictures going upwards below the rail. There was a crimson fitted carpet on the hall and going up the stairs and the light fitting was triple-stalked in some fake brassy material.

I went into the scullery.

On either side of the chimney breast he'd built units in tongue and groove. On one side there was the T.V. neatly boxed in and some little open compartments with things like framed photos and glass ornaments and fruit bowls in them. One compartment had newspapers the *T.V. Times* and the *Radio Times* neatly slotted into it. The unit on the other side was for his books.

There were rows of *Reader's Digest*, of *Wide World*, of *Argosy*, of *Real Male*, of *Guns illustrated*, of *Practical Handyman*, of *Canadian Star Weekly*, of *National Geo-*

graphic. They were all on the bottom shelves. Above were the paperbacks. There was Luke Short and Max Brand and J.T. Edson and Louis L'amour. There was Russell Braddon and W.B. Thomas and Guy Gibson. There was Victor Canning and Alistair Maclean and Ewart Brookes and Ian Fleming. There was Bill Bowes and Stanley Matthews and Bobby Charlton. There was Barbara Tuchman and Winston Churchill and General Patton and Audie Murphy. Above these were his records. Band of the Coldstream Guards, Eric Coates, Stan Kenton, Ray Anthony, Mel Torme, Frankie Laine, Ted Heath, This is Hancock, Vaughan Williams.

His slippers were on the tiled hearth. A black leather swivel chair was angled to face in the direction of the television.

There was no fire in the grate.

I looked through into the kitchen. It was tidy. The cherry red formica-faced sink unit had been given a wash down. There was no rubbish in the rubbish bucket. There was an empty dog bowl on the floor.

I went back into the scullery and opened the adjoining door to the front room. On the mantelpiece there was a small lamp with a crimson shade and I switched it on.

There were not many flowers. There was my wreath, and a lot of flowers from Margaret, and another wreath from Doreen.

The head of the coffin was dead centre to the middle of the bay window and the coffin cut the room in half. Next to the coffin and facing it was a dining-room chair. I went over to where the chair was and looked into the coffin. I hadn't seen him for such a long time. Death didn't really make much difference at all; the face just re-assembled the particles of memory. And as usual when you see someone dead who you've seen alive it was impossible to imagine the corpse as being related to its former occupant. It had that porcelain look about it. I felt that if I tapped it on the forehead with my knuckle there would be a pinging sound.

'Well, Frank,' I said. 'Well, well.'

I stood there for a bit longer then sat down in the dining chair.

I said a few words although I don't know what I said and bowed my head on the edge of the casket for a few minutes then I sat up and undid my coat and took out my fags. I lit up and blew out the smoke slowly and looked at the last of Frank.

Looking at him I found it hard to realise I'd ever known him. All the things about him that I remembered in my mind's eye didn't seem real. They seemed like bits of a film. And even when I saw myself in the flashbacks, as you do, you get outside yourself, I didn't seem real either, neither did the settings or the colours or the way the clouds rushed across the sky while we were doing something particular underneath them.

I took the flask out and had a pull. I looked back at Frank. I stayed there for a minute, looking at him like that, then I screwed the cap back on and walked into the scullery closing the door behind me.

I went into the hall and up the stairs. I opened the first door on the landing. It was Doreen's room. It used to be mine and Frank's. The wallpaper had guitars and musical notes and microphones as a pattern. There were pictures of the Beatles, and the Moody Blues, and the Tremeloes and Dave Dee, Dozy, Beaky, Mick and Titch; centre-spreads from beat magazines Sellotaped on the walls. There were records and a record player in a cupboard unit next to her single bed which was made up to look like a divan, pushed against one wall. There was a whitewood dressing table opposite the bed and next to that a rod and curtain across the corner made a wardrobe. A drawer of the dressing table was open and a stocking was hanging out. I went into Frank's room. It used to be Mam and Dad's. There was a pre-war bed and a pre-war tallboy and a pre-war wardrobe and patterned lino on the floor. Everything was very tidy. On the mantelpiece was a framed photograph of me and Frank as lads in our best suits outside the Salvation Army. We hadn't been Salvationists but we used to go on Sunday mornings and sing because we used to enjoy it as a change.

I sat down on Frank's bed and it creaked and sagged. The lino was green and cold. I dropped my cigarette on the floor and put my foot on it. I sat there for quite a time before I went downstairs and got my hold-all and brought it back upstairs with me.

I began to get ready for bed when I remembered something. I looked round the room and wondered if he'd kept it. Why should he? But then, why should he give it away? I walked over to the wardrobe and opened the door just on the off-chance.

The stock gleamed beneath the hanging line of Frank's clothes. I squatted down and reached inside and took hold of it just above the trigger. The barrel clattered against the back of the wardrobe. The sound was hollow and it echoed coldly on the patterned lino. I pulled the gun out of the wardrobe. Where the stock had been, tucked behind a pair of shoes, there was a box of cartridges. I took that out too. I carried the gun and the box over to the bed and sat down again.

I looked at the gun. Christ, we'd sweated to save up for it. Nearly two years, both of us. No pictures, no football, no fireworks. We'd made a pact: if one of us broke it, the other was to take all the money and spend it on whatever he wanted. I knew Frank wouldn't break the pact. But I thought I might. And so did he. Somehow, though, I'd stuck to it.

And then we'd sweated when we'd finally got it. Sweated in case our dad ever found out. He would have broken it in two and made us watch him do it. We used to keep it round Nezzer Eyres's and pick it up on Sundays when we wanted it. But once we'd collected it we never felt safe until we'd biked at least half a dozen streets away from Jackson Street.

We used to take turns at carrying it. When it was my turn, I always used to think my time went quicker than when Frank was carrying it. We went all over with it. Back Hill, Sanderson's Flats, Fallow Fields. But the best place was the river bank. It was a nine mile bike ride but it was worth it. The river was broad, two miles in parts and the banks were always deserted, and we used to like it best in winter when the wind raced up the estuary under the broad grey sky, and we were all wrapped up, striding along in front of the wind, carrying the gun, popping it off at nothing.

Those times were the best times I ever had as a lad. Just alone with Frank down on the river. But that was before he'd begun to hate my guts.

Not that I'd exactly been full of brotherly love for him before I'd left the town.

He'd been so fucking po-faced about

everything. Siding with our dad all the time, although never hardly saying anything. He'd just let me know by the way he'd looked at me. Maybe that's why I'd hated him sometimes; I could tell how right about me he'd thought he was. Well, he *was* right. So bloody what? There'd been no need for him to be that way. I'd been the same person after he'd started hating me as before. It was just that he'd got to know a few things. And just because he didn't see them my way that was it as far as I was concerned. The less said about me and to me the better. He couldn't see that the dust-up I'd had with our dad was mainly because of the way Frank was towards me.

But all that was past history. As dead as Frank. Nothing could be done about it now. But there were some things that I'd be able to put straight. Just for the sake of the past history.

Friday

I could tell it was windy out before I could hear the wind. It was the daylight, what bit that was getting through the cracks of the curtains. I knew it was windy because of the kind of daylight it was.

33

I rolled on to my back and looked at my watch. It was quarter-to eight. I reached out and grabbed a fag and smoked it looking up at the reflected light on the ceiling getting depressed with the greeny brown gloom, getting impatient with myself for not getting up but laying there anyway, just smoking, balancing the packet on my chest for an ashtray.

Finally I swung out of bed and went into the cold bathroom and got ready for the day. The wind swished about outside beyond the bright frosted glass.

I went downstairs and switched on the wireless. While Family Choice warmed up I went into the kitchen and found the tea caddy and put the kettle on the gas. I made the tea and began to put my cufflinks in.

The back door opened and Doreen came in. She was wearing a black coat, a nice looking one, short, and she had something on the Garbo lines on her head. Her pale gold hair was long and some of it was placed so that it fell down in front of her shoulders, between her shoulders and neck, almost on her breasts.

She looked at me for a minute before shutting the door. After she'd shut it she didn't move except to take her hat off and put it on the drainer and then just stood there with her hands in her high pockets and feet together looking at the floor. She looked more bad tempered than unhappy.

I finished doing my cufflinks.

'Hello, Doreen,' I said.

''lo,' she said.

'How are you feeling?' I said.

'How do you think?'

I began to pour out the tea.

'I'm very sorry about your dad,' I said. She didn't say anything. I offered her a cup of tea but she turned away.

'Enjoying the music, are you?' she said.

'The house seemed cold,' I said. 'Besides...' She shrugged and went into the scullery and sat down on Frank's chair, her hands still in her pockets, her feet still together. I followed her in and sat on the arm of the divan, sipping my tea.

'I really am sorry, Doreen,' I said. 'He was my brother, you know.'

She didn't say anything.

'I don't know what to say,' I said.

Silence.

I didn't want to ask her anything out right before the funeral so I said:

'I couldn't believe it. I just couldn't believe it. He was always so careful.'

Silence.

'I mean, he only drank halves.'

Silence.

'And not turning up for work.'

Two tears began rolling down Doreen's face.

'He wasn't worried about anything, was he? I mean, something on his mind, like, that'd make him careless, through worry, like.'

Silence. The tears rolled further.

'Doreen?'

She whirled up out of the chair.

'Shut up,' she shouted, the tears coming faster. 'Shut up. I can't bear it.'

She ran into the kitchen and stopped in front of the sink, head bowed, shoulders heaving, her arms by her side.

'Can't bear what, love?' I said standing behind her. 'What is it you can't bear?'

'Me dad,' she said. 'Me dad. He's bloody dead, isn't he?' She turned towards me. 'Isn't he?'

I put my arms up and she fell against me. I pressed her to me and let her get it over with.

After a while she straightened up and I poured her a fresh cup of tea. This time she took it. I sat down on the red leatherette topped high stool next to the sink unit and watched her alternately drinking out of and looking into the cup. I wondered if it had all been just because her dad was dead through in the front room or was there something else. I couldn't really tell. Last time I saw her was eight years ago and then she'd been seven so I didn't know what she was like. I could guess though.

She was older than her fifteen natural years. I could have fancied her myself if she hadn't been who she was. You could tell she knew what was what. It's all in the eyes. I wondered if Frank had known she was no virgin. Probably, but he'd never have let on to himself. And if anything had been worrying him he wouldn't have let on to her either. That was the way Frank was. So there was no reason why she should know anything unless she'd seen something or heard something that Frank didn't know she heard. If she had I'd find out, but not today.

I got off the stool and went into the scullery and turned the wireless off. It was half-past eight. Outside, a milk trolley was whirring by. I went back into the kitchen.

'Would you like a fag?' I said.

She nodded and put the cup down. I lit us up. She didn't smoke too badly even though she was conscious of it. After a few drags, I said:

'What do you intend doing now?'

'I dunno.'

'Well, you won't be staying here, will you?'

She shook her head.

'Look,' I said, 'I know you don't know me very well and what you do know you don't like, but I'm going to suggest something to you. You probably won't be very keen on the idea, but I want you to think about it over the next few days: I'm off to South Africa next week. With a woman I may or may not end up marrying. We're flying on Wednesday. I've got three tickets. Why don't you come with us?'

She looked at me. I couldn't tell what she was thinking.

'Think about it. I'd like you to come. If only to square certain things with your dad.'

'Charming,' she said. 'You make me feel real wanted.'

'I'll be here all over the weekend,' I said. 'So you've time to think about it.'

'No thanks.'

She carried on looking at me. I looked at my watch.

'They'll be here at quarter to,' I said. 'Do you want five minutes with him before they come?'

She looked away. She was her fifteen years again.

'No.'

'He'd want it,' I said.

She sobbed, once.

'Go on,' I said. 'You've just time.'

She put her cigarette down on her saucer and went through. Five minutes later she came out. Her face was wet and her eyes were red.

I put my jacket on and went into the front room. I stood next to the casket. The face looked up at the ceiling. There was never anything so still as that face.

I heard a motor outside and then there was a knock at the door.

'Ta-ra, Frank,' I said.

I turned away and walked out of the room via the door that led into the hall. I opened the front door. The man in the tall hat was there.

'Good morning, sir,' he said, in that voice they all have.

We left the church and got into the car again. Doreen and I got into the back and the Vicar got in next to the driver. We drove along the back streets. At one point an old josser on a bike just as old gave us right of way at a junction and slowly and gravely raised his hat.

After a bit the Vicar leant his arm on the back of his seat and looking around him said:

'You'll see some changes in the town since you've been away, Mr Carter.'

'A few,' I said.

'Yes,' he said. 'Things are changing. But not quickly enough to my mind. One day, though, all this will be gone. And then, thank heaven, people will have somewhere decent to bring up their children. Somewhere they'll want to go home to instead of the street.'

I said: 'Always assuming what they replace it with will be better.'

'Oh,' he said, 'but it must be. It's bound to be.'

'Is it?' I said.

I looked at him. He had sandy hair and glasses and a yellow face. It was impossible to tell how old he was.

We rolled down the hill to the cemetery. The day was bright and windy and low grey fluffy clouds raced across the thin sun.

At the graveside apart from the Vicar and the digger and the undertaker's men there was me and Doreen and two blokes who'd been waiting near where the coffin had been unloaded. One of them was about fifty, the other about twenty-two or three. They looked like barmen and no mistake. They were neatest around the neck, with their clean white collars and neat knots, but the smartness tapered off the lower down their bodies you got and they were scruffiest round their feet. They stood there with their heads bowed and their hands clasped in front of them, a bit behind me and Doreen.

I held her hand while the Vicar said the words. The grave-digger was unshaven and wore a big ex-army greatcoat with the collar turned up and all through the Vicar's spiel he kept looking at Doreen, the dirty old sod.

'Ashes to ashes, dust to dust...'

I reached down and picked up a handful of earth and gave some to Doreen. The barmen stepped forward and got some as well and we showered the lowering coffin. The barmen stepped back. The older one put his hand to his mouth and coughed and stood to attention and the younger one shot his cuffs.

The Vicar led us into *Rock of Ages*. Doreen got past the first few words then shook and didn't sing any more. The grave-digger went to work with his shovel. Wind whistled through my black mohair. A dozen or so rows away two middle-aged women in grey hats paused to watch as they picked their way among the headstones.

And then that was it.

I guided Doreen away from the grave. She stumbled as she took one look back at what she didn't understand. The barmen stepped back to let us by. I nodded to them.

We got to the cars. I looked towards the gates. A woman with blonde hair wearing a bright green belted coat was standing beyond the railings.

'Is that Margaret?' I said.

Doreen nodded.

I looked across at the woman. She didn't move. Doreen got in the car still crying.

'Hang on a minute,' I said. I turned to the barmen who were walking in the direction

41

of the cars, lighting up.

'Can you wait?' I called.

They looked at one another. The older one looked at his watch and nodded. I walked over to the gates. Margaret was still there and she didn't attempt to move. She wasn't bad looking. The only thing being that she looked exactly what she was: a singing room belle.

'I thought you said you weren't coming,' I said.

'I changed me mind,' she said.

There was a trace of a London accent on top of her broad Northern.

'I'm glad,' I said. 'I want to talk to you.'

'What about?'

'Doreen,' I lied.

She looked across to the waiting cars.

'Did – did everything go off all right?' she said.

'Fine. The arrangements were fine. Thanks.'

Her eyes were just as wet as those sort of eyes will ever be.

'I want to talk to you,' I said again.

She carried on looking at the cars.

'How's Doreen?'

'How'd you expect?' I said. 'She know about you and Frank?'

Margaret gave me a smile that meant she thought I had something missing.

'She knew. Why shouldn't she?'

'Because, like, I was thinking, can't you come back with us? Now? I mean, Doreen needs somebody and I'm not much use.'

She shook her head.

'I can't,' she said, 'so don't ask.'

'Well, when? I mean, I've got to settle up things before I go back. How about later on?'

'No,' she said.

'Sometime tomorrow?'

She looked at me.

'All right,' she said. 'Tomorrow morning. In "The Cecil" at twelve.'

'That's where Frank worked,' I said.

'I know,' she said. 'I go there because it's a long walk for me husband from where we live.'

'All right,' I said. 'I'll see you tomorrow.'

She turned and began to walk away.

I watched her for a minute then I went back into the cemetery.

I opened the front door. Doreen went in first and the two barmen followed. In the hall Doreen took her hat off.

'Go through,' I said to the blokes. 'I shan't be a minute.'

I went upstairs and got some ginger ales and two bottles of scotch out of my hold-all. When I got downstairs Doreen was in the kitchen and the two blokes were standing in front of the fireplace lighting up again.

'Will this do?' I said, holding up the bottle.

'Oh, well,' said the older one, 'thanks very much.'

'Ta,' said the younger one.

They tried to look solemn and appreciative at the same time.

I went through into the kitchen. Doreen was making some tea.

'Doreen, love,' I said, 'could you tell me where there's any glasses, please?'

She indicated a cabinet. I took out the glasses and began pouring the scotch.

'How long are they going to be?' she said.

'I don't know, love,' I said. 'Not long.'

I took the top off a ginger ale and filled a small jug with water.

'Will you have one?' I said. 'It'll do you good.'

Doreen took a long look at the bottle then got hold of it and poured herself some. She took it straight back and made a face and then stared into the bottom of the glass. I poured three large ones and took them through.

'Water or ginger?' I said.

It was water for the older one and ginger for the younger one.

I went back into the kitchen. Doreen had taken another drink.

'Are you going to join us?' I said.

She shook her head. I put my hand on her shoulder.

'Suit yourself, love,' I said. 'Just do what you want.'

I went through again. I put the ginger and the jug and the bottle I'd opened on the low table in front of the divan.

'Dig in,' I said.

They helped themselves.

'Absent friends,' I said.

'Absent friends,' they said.

We drank.

The older one was called Eddie Appleyard. He had frizzy black hair, quite long; brushed straight back from his forehead and long sideboards that spread across his cheeks in whispy patches that were turning grey. He had false teeth that didn't fit properly. He was a local.

The younger one was called Keith Lacey. He had the face and build of a young footballer. The face was flat the body compact and stocky. His hair was fair and it had been curly before he'd had it given a crew cut. He wore a gold ring on the third finger of his left hand. He was from Liverpool.

I filled up the glasses.

'Well,' I said. 'I'd like to say thanks for coming.'

'Don't thank us Mr Carter,' said Eddie. 'Frank was a good bloke.'

'He was that,' said Keith.

'One of the best,' said Eddie.

'How long had you known him?' I said.

'Me?' said Eddie. 'We first got pally when we was working at Lingholme working men's club. That were, oh, five, six year ago. We got on more or less right from the start like. I left about a year after, went to "Crown and Anchor", but we used to see each other on Saturdays. He'd changed his job as well and neither of us was far from ground and we used to meet outside at half-past three after we'd done siding up. We'd buy a couple of hot pies outside and take 'em in ground with us and we'd have missed about half-an-hour of game but we always used to go. Never missed a game, not even when they went down to third division for a bit.'

'Aye,' I said, 'he liked his football, did Frank. We always used to go when we was kids.'

'I couldn't believe it when I heard,' said Keith. 'I mean, I was surprised when he didn't turn up for evening session, because like, Frank was always on time, always first in. But when I heard, I mean, I couldn't understand it. I mean, Frank only drank halves. And he always used to say that whenever he went out for a drink he'd always leave his car behind so's he could enjoy himself.'

'I know,' I said. 'Frank was always careful.'

There was a silence.

46

'I still can't believe it,' said Keith.

We all drank. I moved the bottle round again.

'Everybody liked Frank,' said Eddie.

There was more silence.

'He always spoke well of you, Mr Carter,' said Keith. 'He always said he admired you for getting on so well.'

Frank had always said that to people. Perhaps he'd even got so he thought that way himself.

'It's a bloody funny thing, though,' said Eddie. 'I mean, you know a bloke for six bloody years and all the time he's as calm as Gentle Jesus, never touches the hard stuff and then he goes off and drinks a bottle of fucking whisky and drives himself off top road and finishes up in three feet of water. It's not right, you know, it's not bloody right.' He took a quick drink. 'It shouldn't have happened. Not to a bloke like Frank. He was one of the best.'

His eyes were getting watery. He fumbled a fag into his mouth and I poured some more scotch. Eddie couldn't find his matches so I lit him up.

'Thanks,' he said, from the back of his throat. Whether it was the scotch or genuine feeling that was breaking Eddie up didn't really matter because whichever way it was, right now Eddie believed completely in the sincerity of his words.

47

Nobody said anything for a while. Then I said:

'You don't think he might have done it on purpose?'

They looked at me.

'What? You mean, like, killed himself?' said Keith.

I didn't say anything.

Keith turned his head slightly to one side then looked back at me, a grotesque half smile on his face.

'Naw,' he said. 'Frank? Kill himself? You what?'

I carried on looking at him. He looked back at me, incredulous.

'I mean, what for?'

'That's what I was wondering,' I said.

'Come off,' he said. 'I mean, Frank was … was … well … I mean … he wasn't the bloke to get into a mess or owt, something he couldn't see the way out of. And he'd no worries, I know. I mean, I would have known. Hell, we worked together every day for the last year. It would have showed.'

'Why would it?'

'Well, it just would. I mean, he was always the same. Always. Never any different.'

'What was he like when you saw him last?'

'Sunday? Just the same. On time. Worked hard. You know.'

Eddie poured himself a large one.

'And there was nothing he did to make

48

you think maybe something was up?'

'Naw, nothing. I tell you, he was just the same.'

'And you don't suppose something could have happened between when you saw him and when he started getting drunk?'

'Well, I don't know. I suppose so. But it'd have to be something awful. And what happened that's awful?'

'I don't know,' I said.

'I mean, you'd know if something had.'

'I don't know,' I said.

Eddie was pouring another drink. He seemed to have left the conversation a few drinks back.

'Bloody good bloke,' he said. 'One of the best.'

'How the fuckin' hell would you know, you old pissarse,' shrieked Doreen.

She was standing in the doorway, glass in hand. Behind her I could see the bottle I'd left on the sink. It was well down. Tears were streaming down her face. Her coat was undone.

'How would you know?' she shrieked again, this time a little lower pitched. 'Or you? Or you? Especially you,' she said to me. 'None of you knew. I knew. He was me dad.'

The last word was a terrible scream and as she screamed it she flung the glass in the direction of Eddie although I'm pretty sure she wasn't aiming at anyone in particular.

The glass hit Eddie on his shoulder and whisky went all over his sleeve. He leapt up out of his seat. I moved towards Doreen. Keith stood up, still holding his glass.

'Now, Doreen, love,' I said.

'Get away,' she said. 'Get away from me.'

'Look,' I said. 'I know how you feel and...'

'No you don't, no you don't. If you did you'd leave me alone!'

She ran over to the door that led into the hall and pulled it open.

'Come on,' she said. 'Clear off! Clear off, the lot of you!'

I nodded to the others. They drank up and began to walk out. Eddie was dabbing at his sleeve with his handkerchief.

'Hang about,' I said. 'I'll be out in a sec.'

When they'd gone I was about to say something to Doreen but she rushed away from the door and flung herself down in Frank's chair, her fist pressed against her lips, her legs drawn up underneath her. She began to cry again.

'Look,' I said, 'if I was you I'd go and have a lie down for a bit.'

She didn't answer.

'I've got to go out for an hour,' I said, 'but I'll be back later.'

Nothing.

I looked at her for a minute or two and then went out, closing the door quietly behind me.

They were standing on the pavement, by the gate. Eddie was still dabbing away. They looked at me as I came out.

'Sorry about that,' I said, closing the gate. 'She's taking it bad.'

'Oh, Christ,' said Keith, 'don't worry about it. I mean she's upset, isn't she?'

'Yes,' said Eddie, 'poor old lass.'

I took a quid out of my wallet.

'Here,' I said. 'This is for the dry cleaning.'

'Oh no, Mr Carter,' he said. 'I couldn't do that.'

But I knew he could and eventually he did.

'Anyway,' I said, 'let's go and have a drink.'

Eddie looked at his watch.

'I can't very well,' he said. 'I've got to be at work in twenty minutes.'

'How about you?' I said to Keith.

'I'm all right. I'm not on till six.'

Eddie said: 'Well I'll be off then.'

There was regret in his voice. He was sad about missing the forthcoming whiskies.

I shook hands with him.

'Thanks for coming,' I said. 'I appreciate it.'

He became emotional again.

'It's the least I could have done,' he said. 'Frank was a good bloke. One of the best.'

'Yes,' I said.

We all stood there for a minute.

'Anyway,' said Eddie.

51

He shook my hand again and turned away and began to cross the road, diagonally making for the end of the street, his hands in his pockets, his jacket unbuttoned and blowing behind him in the breeze.

I turned to Keith.

'Come on,' I said.

We walked along the street in the opposite direction to the way Eddie had gone.

The corner of Jackson Street and Park Street, the street that led back to the High Street was about twenty yards from the railings at the bottom. Keith automatically began to turn the corner but when he saw I was carrying on to the bottom he stopped and wandered down after me.

I stood by the railings and looked across the remains of the grass to where the dyke used to be. A couple of blokes from the engineering works were carrying a packing case into the building. The lathe droned on.

Keith was standing behind me.

'What's up?' he said.

'Nowt,' I said. 'Just having a look.'

On the way to 'The Cecil' I made a phone call. Keith waited outside the box, leaning against the post office wall.

When I got through Audrey's voice said:

'Hello, Audrey Fletcher speaking?'

That meant Gerald was there.

'I'll call back,' I said. 'Tell Gerald it was a wrong number.'

'I'm sorry, I think you must have the wrong number.'

'You've got a lovely pair of titties,' I said.

'That's quite all right,' she said and put the phone down. We walked into 'The Cecil'.

I'd remembered it very well, considering it must have been twelve years since I'd been inside it.

When I was a kid, when I'd started going in pubs, they'd said you want to keep out of 'The Cecil', you don't want to be going there, it's rough, especially Saturday, it's the worst pub in town. Somebody had once said they should advertise it as having 'Singing till ten, fighting till eleven'. So naturally I started going in there as soon as they'd let me get up to the bar. One of the first times I'd ever been in, it was a Friday, everything had been all right, nobody seemed to be looking for anything and I'd gone for a slash, and when I'd come out again, there was a great space cleared in front of the bar, all the tables had been pushed back from it, everybody was standing up, some on tables or chairs, all holding their drinks and it was very quiet. In front of the bar in the space that'd been cleared there were eight blokes, standing facing the bar, all holding bottles or broken glasses, and standing on the bar top were the barmen, about a dozen of them, all facing the blokes, all holding bum starters, ready for it.

The main bar was one of the biggest I've ever been in. You go in through the double doors that open on to the High Street, and first off all you see are tables, hundreds of round tables, set out in rows going diagonally across the room, stretching as far back as you can see. Beyond the tables, it seems like a hundred yards away, there's the stage, a long low platform and on it a set of drums, a piano and a Hammond organ with all the attachments. Running down the left hand wall as you look from the entrance is the bar. There are eight sets of pumps. The bar stops flush with the stage. It's that long.

Between the tables and the entrance there is a strip of carpet about twelve feet wide. It runs along the top end of the room, flush to the bar seats beneath the windows. Against the bar seats are more tables, just one row, five either side of the door, following the carpet from the bar to the right hand wall. These tables are where you sit at dinner time, so that the main mass of tables remain clean and polished for the evening when they have singing and comedians and strippers and fights.

Keith and I walked across the carpet to the bar. There were three barmen on duty. So far we were the only customers.

The nearest barman moved towards us. He looked at Keith and nodded.

'Hello, Keith,' he said.

'Now then,' said Keith.

I took my wallet out.

'Yes, sir,' said the barman.

'What do you want Keith?' I said.

'Pint of bitter, please,' he said.

'Two pints and two large scotches,' I said. 'Bell's if you've got it.'

'Right you are, sir,' he said and moved across to the nearest pumps.

'Thanks very much,' said Keith.

'Does he know where you've been?' I said, indicating the barman.

'Yes.'

'How is it he didn't come?'

'He's only been here a week today. He only met Frank twice.'

'What about any of the others?'

Keith shrugged.

'I dunno. A couple of 'em said they'd try and make it. But what with it being either their time off, or else working, you know.'

He looked a bit embarrassed.

'So Frank wasn't all that popular,' I said.

'I wouldn't say that. He kept himself to himself. You know.'

'What did he do, work too hard for their bloody liking?'

Keith shrugged again and frowned and there was a touch of red on his cheeks.

The barman came back with the drinks.

'Anything with the scotch, sir?' he said.

'A ginger ale,' I said. 'How much is that?'

'Fifteen and five, sir.'

'Will you have one?'

'Oh well, that's very kind of you sir, I'll have a Mackeson if I might.'

He took for the drinks and we carried them over to a table near the door. I drank the scotch and took a sip of beer. Keith gave me a fag and we lit up. Beyond the smoked glass traffic droned up and down the High Street. Occasionally the wind rattled the double doors.

'Keith,' I said, 'how friendly were you and Frank?'

He scratched the skin between his nostrils and his upper lip.

'Well, you know, like I said. We worked together. I'd known him twelve months. Ever since I worked here.'

'Yes,' I said. 'I know. But how well did you know him?'

He frowned.

'Well, we sort of used to talk when it was quiet, you know about football and the general state of affairs in the world, things like that.'

'Did you ever go back home with him?'

'Oh no. This was during working time.'

'You never went drinking with him or owt like that?'

'Naw. Nowt like that. I once bumped into him in "The Crown", and had a couple with him, but it was only accidental.'

56

'Who was he with?'

'His girl friend, Margaret.'

'Did he ever talk to you about her?'

'No.'

'How is it you know who she is?'

He looked at me, sideways, wondering.

'Well, she's fairly well known. Round the pubs like.'

I took a drag.

'I'd say she was a whore,' I said. 'What would you say?'

He gave me that look again.

'Well, I don't know.'

'Come off it,' I said.

'Well, yeah, I'd say so.'

'And everybody knew she was a whore, didn't they?'

'I expect so.'

'You know it,' I said. 'Did Frank know it?'

He took a drink.

'I don't know.'

'And if he didn't, you didn't bother to tell him?'

'Well, you can't, can you? Anyway, he must have known. She doesn't exactly hide her light under a bushel.'

'Right,' I said. 'Right.'

I took a long drink of beer.

'Did Frank ever talk to you about his missus?'

'No.'

'Did you know he had one?'

'Well, I guessed. Because of the kid, like.'

'Did you know Doreen, then?'

'Today was the first time I ever saw her.'

'Frank told you about her?'

'Yes.'

'What did he say about her?'

'Well, you know, he'd tell me what he'd been doing for her. Fixing up her bedroom. Papering the hall because she wanted it brightening up. Things like that. He liked to talk about her.'

'She was all he bloody well had,' I said.

Keith took a long drink of beer, watching me all the time.

'Shall I tell you something?' I said.

Keith said nothing.

'His wife, Frank's, she was one of those women you see shopping in the street, with her shopping bag and her headscarf and her glasses and her fag on all the time. She was plain as buggery. She even used to look like it before she was married. She looked as if she'd let herself give it to Frank once, on their wedding night, and after that he could whistle. I remember she always wore her glasses and she only needed them for reading. But Frank married her.'

Keith kept on looking at me.

'And do you know what happened? Some wogs moved into the house down the street. Pakistanis. One day Frank gashed his hand on a glass at work and had to go to hospital to get some stitches put in. He called in at home after. Only she wasn't there. He went out of the house to see if she was coming down the street but there was no signs. He was just going back in when he saw her coming out of the wogs place. He couldn't grasp it at first until she saw him and started to run off down the street. Then he knew all right. He caught her and dragged her back home and beat the shit out of her. A few days later the wogs left, went to Leeds or somewhere. And she went with them. That was when Doreen was seven.'

'Hell,' said Keith. 'No wonder he never said owt about her.'

'Do you know what she did?' I said. 'After?'

'What?' said Keith.

'A few days after she left she sent Frank a letter. He got it the day of our dad's funeral. I was up for it. In the letter she called Frank everything she could think of. She finished up saying that Doreen wasn't Frank's kid. She said that I was Doreen's father. She said it because she knew how much Frank thought about Doreen.'

'Christ,' said Keith.

'Frank showed me the letter,' I said. 'He was very calm about it. He stood there while I read it and then he just said "Jack, I don't ever want to see you in this house again". I mean, he'd had the letter from the day before. He'd had time to do all sorts of things. Get drunk, go for me, anything. But he held it all back. He just told me he didn't want anything else to do with me and that was that.'

'So he believed her then?'

I nodded.

'It wasn't true though?'

'I don't know,' I said.

Keith looked at me.

'What I mean is, I had Muriel, ugly as she bloody was, shortly before they were married. I was only twenty-two. Doreen came on the scene eight months after they were wed. So I don't know, do I? I saw her today for the first time in eight years. The time before that she was a baby.'

Keith looked into his beer. I remembered how it had happened. I'd been on my way home from the pub and I'd bumped into Muriel and two of her mates. They'd been pissed as farts. They'd had a hen party on the strength of Muriel's coming wedding. When I'd bumped into them they'd been full of it. Talking dirty, swearing, having me on. There's nobody muckier minded than a pissed-up bird. One of them had lived nearby. She'd said why didn't we all go back to her place for a cup of tea? I'd said all right. I hadn't been sober and I'd quite fancied my chances with one of the birds. When we'd got back there the bird had

60

brought the drinks out and the talk'd got filthier. It'd made me very horny. I'd been sitting in an easy chair and Muriel'd been sitting in one facing me and the other two birds were on the settee. Muriel hadn't been particular about the way she'd been sitting and I'd been able to see right up her legs. Not that I'd been pretending not to. I'd been too far gone for that. One of the birds on the settee had made a joke about it to Muriel and Muriel'd leant across and lifted the skirt of the other bird and'd said something like now we can all see what you've got too. The other bird had done the same back to Muriel and then the two of them had started mucking about trying to shove each other's skirts up to their waists. They'd kept looking at me and screeching and laughing all the time it'd gone on. They'd been so pissed they hadn't even tried to keep the noise down. The third bird'd joined in and between them they'd pinned Muriel down on the settee and whipped her drawers off. One of the birds'd danced round the room waving them in the air while Muriel'd tried to get them back off her. Eventually the third bird'd looked at me and said to the others something like why should he be getting to see everything? Why should he have all the fun? Let's have a look at his. The two other birds had jumped on me and started unbuttoning my flies. Muriel'd

61

staggered over and joined in. I hadn't actually tried to put up a lot of resistance. Anyway, at that point, somebody knocked on the front door and the bird who'd lived there had gone to see who it was. I'd fastened up just in case. I'd thought it might have been the birds folks coming home. It'd been some neighbour on about the noise. The bird and the neighbour'd started having a ding-dong on the steps. While that'd been going on the third bird'd started feeling sick and she'd cleared off to the lav. That'd left me and Muriel. She'd come and sat on the arm of the chair and started unbuttoning me again, making sure I was seeing everything she'd got. The front door'd slammed but the bird hadn't come back in the room because the third bird'd started puking all up the stair carpet.

It'd been all over in five minutes. We'd laid down on the carpet and the minute I'd put it in her I'd come. And the minute I'd come I'd started to feel fucking awful. I'd wanted to cry and beat my fists on the floor and be sick but all Muriel had been doing was bloody cursing because it was all over. I remember I'd got up off her and I'd started cursing her at the top of my voice. The knocking had started again on the front door and the bird whose place it was had come in to see what I was on about. Finally I'd just run out past her, out of the front door past the old bugger who'd been doing the complaining.

I'd known I wouldn't be able to face Frank, not when the wedding was only a week off. I'd been living at Albert's at the time because our dad wouldn't have me in the house. Neither Frank nor our dad had known where I was so it was easy for me not to turn up at the wedding. I only saw Muriel once after that. The night I half killed our dad. Frank and her had lived at Jackson Street and when I saw her I couldn't believe it had happened. She'd never looked anything at all but seeing her there with her hair in curlers and her fag on and no make-up made me almost think I'd dreamt it. But I hadn't.

When I found out Frank'd got a daughter it never clicked that it could have been mine. Maybe I'd brainwashed myself about that night to the point where I couldn't let any thought like that into my mind. Even when Frank showed me the letter at our dad's funeral I wouldn't admit it to myself. I never had done. Not even now. Doreen was Frank's. What had happened between me and Muriel had happened. But Doreen was Frank's. She had to be Frank's. He had to have that.

The thing I'd always wondered, though, was whether Frank'd believed Muriel. He believed that me and Muriel had been together. He knew that we were both

63

capable of that. But whether or not he'd believed that Doreen might not be his was another matter. I don't think he allowed himself to believe it. That's the way Frank was. Anything he didn't like he shut out. Like me.

'So, like I was saying,' I said to Keith, 'the one time Frank had a good reason to either kill me or kill Muriel or go crazy one way or another, he just turned himself inside out and asked me if I wouldn't mind leaving the room. If he did drive himself off top road then whatever made him do it was even worse than what he found out about me and Muriel.'

'And Doreen,' said Keith.

I didn't pass any remark at what Keith said.

'But,' I said, 'I doubt if he did it on purpose.'

'So do I,' said Keith. 'As you say, Frank wasn't the type.'

'At the same time … Frank wouldn't have got blind pissed on scotch instead of turning up for work, would he?'

'Well, no,' said Keith.

I stubbed out my cigarette.

'Keith,' I said, 'how much do you know about what goes on?'

'How do you mean?'

'Around here. Among the big boys. The governors.'

64

'I don't know nowt, I suppose.'

'But you know that there are governors?'

'I suppose so, yes.'

'Ever met any of them?'

'No.'

'Do you know any of their names?'

'Well, I know there's a bloke called Thorpe.'

'And what does he do?'

'He does loans around steelworks. He has a few blokes who do his collecting for him. They come in here sometimes.'

'And he's a governor, is he?'

Keith didn't say anything. I smiled.

'Do you know who your boss is?'

'Mr Gardner.'

'Who's he?'

'The manager.'

'And who does he work for?'

'Well, this isn't a brewery house, so he works for the company who owns it.'

'Cotel Limited?'

'That's right.'

'They own motels and hotels together with one or two pubs, don't they?'

'That's right.'

'And who owns Cotel Limited?'

'I don't know.'

'No,' I said, 'and you never will. Except that he's a governor. Do you know who Thorpe works for?'

'No.'

'The owner of Cotel Limited. Do you know who runs Greenley's Betting Shops?'

Keith didn't answer.

'Right,' I said. 'You've heard of Wold Haulage Limited?'

He nodded.

'Chap called Marsh runs it, doesn't he?'

Keith nodded again.

'Well, he doesn't. Guess who does? And who owns the wog houses in Jackson Street and Voltaire Road and Linden Street? And the gambling clubs and the brothels and Greaves' Country Pies and Sausages Ltd?'

Keith's cigarette had burned down to the tip. He put it out and got another one from his packet.

'Do you remember a couple of years ago when five Pakistanis got carved up outside of here? On the pavement?'

'I wasn't here then but I heard about it.'

'It said in the papers there were about eighteen of them, all Pakistanis. Fighting among themselves.'

'That's right.'

'Well, what happened, you see, was that some of our coloured friends had started a cheap whorehouse down Clarendon Street. The novelty attracted a lot of customers. Too many. They decided to open up additional premises. That was just before the party on the pavement. Everybody thought it was just what it looked like; too much ale. But what happened was that there was half a dozen Pakistanis from the whorehouse against half a dozen Pakistanis from various properties in Jackson Street and Voltaire Road and Linden Street. Properties owned by a certain person. They were helped by half a dozen gents of the strictly British persuasion. Lots of people saw it but there were no witnesses. The police only arrested the ones who'd been hospitalised. For some reason or other they were satisfied with the ones they'd got. Anyway, you'll gather that after that nobody else bothered to try and open up in competition.'

Keith was watching me, wondering how I knew about it all.

'It was in all the papers. I guessed that something of this sort was going on, so I rang Frank up. Just to see if he was all right, in one way or another. Frank had a good idea that it wasn't the way it looked, but he wasn't saying anything. Frank wouldn't get involved in owt like that for all the tea in China. He always played safe. But he knew. He always knew what was going on.'

I looked at Keith.

'You see, the only way Frank could get into trouble was if he'd heard something and told somebody else about it. But he wouldn't do that, would he?'

'Well, no,' said Keith.

67

'So he wasn't the kind of bloke to get pissed and accidentally drive himself off top road. He wasn't the kind of bloke to do it on purpose. And he wasn't the kind of bloke to get into trouble with some people that might matter. So what?'

The doors were pushed open and three steelworkers came in, carrying their knapsacks. They all looked clean, so that meant they were coming in for a morning session before they went on two to ten.

Keith said: 'I dunno. What?'

'There's only one way Frank'd get mixed up in anything; that's if he saw something he didn't want to see. If that happened, then whatever he saw would have to be pretty dicey. Wouldn't you say?'

'I would. But...'

'But what?'

'Well, what you're saying is that Frank ... Frank was knocked off. I mean definitely.'

'He was.'

'But how can you say that?'

'Because I know it.'

'But how?'

'Because of the line of business I'm in.'

I watched him while that sank in.

'That's why I'm sure, matey,' I said. 'That's why I'm sure.' I drained my glass. 'Shall we have another?'

When he came back from the bar he'd had

time to think about everything I'd said, which was the idea. I'd had time to think too. Now was the time to see if I was right or not.

He put the drinks down.

'Cheers,' I said.

'Cheers,' he said.

I drank the scotch off.

'So believing that, Keith,' I said, 'what do you think I should do? Go to the scuffers?'

I smiled as I said it. He didn't say anything.

I stopped smiling.

'I want you to do something for me,' I said.

He still didn't say anything.

'I want you to keep your eyes and ears open. I want to know anything you hear at the bar. I want to know who says what. About business, about Frank, me, anything. And if anybody asks where I'm staying I want to know that most of all. As soon as you hear that, you put your coat on and walk out of the pub and you come over to 17, Holden Street and tell me. There's money in it to take care of you till you get another job.'

'Yeah,' he said, 'but…'

'But what?'

'It's a bit dicey, isn't it? I mean, what if they know I've been to funeral and met you?'

'Oh, they'll know that,' I said. 'You can count on it.'

69

'Well, there you are. I mean, if I tell on them to you, I'll be in for it, won't I?'

'No,' I lied, 'course not. It's me they'll want. They'll leave you alone. If they touched you it'd be more trouble for them than it's worth.'

'Well...'

'And anyway,' I said, 'I shall be around, in here, so they don't *have* to know where I live. It's just important to me to know who it's important to. You probably won't have to come to where I am. Just tip us the wink when I come in. You know.'

'Well, I suppose so. I mean, if you're in, they don't have to know what we're up to, do they?'

'Course they don't,' I said. 'Course they don't.'

I left Keith at one o'clock picked up the car from the garage in Holden Street and went back to Frank's. Doreen was as I'd left her, except she was asleep. I poured myself a drink and sat down on the divan and waited for her to wake up. I sipped my drink and looked at her. She was well away. You'd have thought she was dead.

Well, if she was mine there was nothing of me there to show for it. There was a lot of Muriel there, but because Doreen was young and looked after herself it didn't matter. I tried to see something of Frank in her but I'd stared at her for too long: She was just a young girl I'd met for the first time that morning. A young girl I'd been to a funeral with.

And now in a way, it didn't matter who she was. If she came to South Africa with me and Audrey then it was up to me to take up where Frank'd left off. Mine or not, like it or not. Whatever she felt about me wouldn't matter all that much: she'd never be short of anything if she came with us. If she came. If she didn't I wasn't going to make her. She could suit herself. I always had done. If she didn't come I'd make arrangements for her to have set amounts of cash from time to time. At least she'd appreciate that. I know I would have done at her age.

She woke up.

She looked at me for a few minutes while she remembered who I was and what had happened.

'How are you feeling now?' I said.

'Lousy,' she said. She moved her tongue about in her dry mouth.

'Would you like another drink?' I said.

She pulled a face.

'Cigarette?'

She shook her head.

I waited for a while.

'Doreen,' I said, 'I know it's not a good time.'

She just stared in front of her at the wall.

71

'But I'm, you know, I'm a bit puzzled. You know, about what happened.'

Nothing.

I leant forward.

'I mean, was your dad worried about anything?'

She shook her head.

'Don't you think he'd have to be, or annoyed or something, to get drunk the way he did?'

'I don't know.'

'Well, something like a row with the boss or something?'

'I didn't see him Sunday night. He was at Margaret's. I was in bed when he got in.'

I took another drink.

'Did you like Margaret?' I said.

'She was all right. She was good fun.'

'You didn't mind what was going on between her and your dad?'

'Why should I?'

I shrugged.

'How do you mean, she was good fun?' I said.

'She just was. When we went out and that.'

'Did you and her ever talk? When Frank wasn't about?'

'What do you mean?'

'Well, just talk.'

'Sometimes.'

'What about?'

'All sorts.'

'Like what?'

'Nothing in particular. She used to tell me what she'd got up to in London and that.'

'When was she in London?'

'I don't know, years ago.'

'What was she doing down there?'

'I don't know.'

'Yes you do.'

'Well, she worked as a hostess or something.'

'Or something. Was she on the game?'

'I didn't ask.'

'Clip joints?'

'I suppose so.'

'And you didn't mind your dad having it off with a slag like her?'

'Look,' she said, 'bloody shut up. Me dad knew what she was like. It was his business. She was all right, was Margaret. She understood things.'

'What things?'

'About life.'

'What about life?'

'She didn't care what everybody thought.'

'In what way.'

'She lived as she pleased.'

'And you agree with her?'

'Well, why not? You're only here once.'

'How many blokes have you had, Doreen.'

'Now look…'

'How many?'

'Mind your bloody business.'

'Did your dad know?'

'Nowt to do with anybody but meself.'

'Did he?'

'Shut up.'

'Do you think he'd have liked it?'

'Shut your mouth.'

'I bet Margaret knew, though. I bet you talked about it with her, didn't you?'

'Why not?'

'I bet you had a right laugh behind his back. I bet he didn't know half of what she was up to, let alone you.'

'She was married. She did as she liked.'

'You sound closer to her than you were to your dad.'

She stood up.

'She understood me,' she said, tears beginning. 'She knew what it was like.'

'Didn't your dad?'

'No.'

'You'll have a better time now he's gone, then, won't you?'

She flew at me. I took hold of her wrists.

'Now listen,' I said. 'Tell me. What was up with your dad? What did he know?'

'Nothing, nothing.'

'I don't believe you. What was wrong?'

'I don't know. Maybe Margaret...'

'What?'

'Maybe she finished with him.'

'And he'd get drunk over that?'

'I don't know.'

'I bet,' I said. 'I bet.'

I pushed her down on to Frank's chair and leaned over her.

'Now, look,' I said. 'It strikes me that for Frank to get drunk the way he did and for him to drive off top road, there must have been something on his mind that was pretty heavy.'

She stared at me.

'Now,' I said, 'I don't know whether it was an accident or on purpose or what. But I'm going to find out. And if it turns out that you know something you're not telling me then I'll knock the living daylights out of you.'

She was frightened to death and at the same time she was bewildered by what I'd said.

'What do you mean?' she said. 'It was an accident. What do you mean?'

I straightened up. So that was it. She didn't know anything.

'What do you mean?' she said again.

'I'll tell you if and when I find out,' I said.

I started to go out of the room and up the stairs. She followed after me.

'What, Uncle Jack?' she said. 'What do you mean?'

'I don't know,' I said, 'so don't ask.'

I went into the bedroom and picked up the hold-all and the shotgun and box of shells.

'But you think…'

'I don't know what I think,' I said.

I walked out of the bedroom and down the stairs. Doreen stood at the top of the stairs.

'Where are you going?'

'To where I'm staying.'

'But what about me dad?'

'I'll let you know what happens.'

'You don't know where I'm staying.'

'I'll find you,' I said.

I closed the front door behind me. I put the hold-all on the front seat and went round to the boot and opened it. I laid the shotgun and the box of shells down on the carpeting. I closed the lid and turned the key in the lock.

I phoned Audrey again. This time Gerald wasn't there.

'Jack,' she said. 'I'm worried.'

'What about?'

'I've been thinking. About what Gerald might do.'

'Don't. He's got to go to the trouble of coming out to Johannesburg himself if he wants you back and I doubt if even you're worth the trouble that'd cause him.'

'But supposing…'

'Listen. I've told you. Stein knows. He'll back me. I'm valuable to him. What I know means money to him. That's what he's paying for.'

There was a silence.

'You know what Gerald would do, don't you? If he ever caught me?'

'Well, he won't because he'd have to do it to me too. So drop it.'

There was another silence.

'Will you be back Sunday?'

'I don't know. You may have to collect the stuff from Maurice yourself if I'm not.'

'When will you let me know?'

'I don't know. Saturday. I'll phone Maurice.'

'What about Doreen?'

'I don't know yet.'

'Do you want her to come with us, Jack?'

'I don't know.'

'I hope you've thought about it, Jack.'

'I've thought,' I said. 'Anyway, I'll phone Saturday.'

'Jack, you'd better be careful. Gerald just might drop you in the cart.'

'I know that. What do you think I am?'

'All right,' she said. 'But try and make it Sunday. You never know.'

'I'll try,' I said and put the receiver down.

I knocked on the door of the boarding house. When she came to the door I said:

'Hello, I hope you don't mind, but I'm a bit earlier than I expected. I hope it's okay.'

'It makes no difference to me,' she said.

'Oh, good,' I said.

I went in and she watched me go up the stairs.

'I expect you'll need some rest,' she said.

I played along with her. I turned at the top of the stairs.

'Well, you know,' I said.

Her face cracked for the first time since we'd met. She obviously liked to think what she was thinking.

'I'm making a cup of tea,' she said. 'Would you like one?'

'Oh, yes, please,' I said. 'That's very kind of you.'

I went into my room and lay down on the bed and lit a cigarette. A few minutes later the door opened. She walked over to the table by the bed and put the tea down. I leaned up on my elbow and took the tea. She sat down on a chair opposite the bed. She folded her arms and crossed her legs. I could see her stocking tops and she knew I could so I looked at them over the top of my tea.

'Ah,' I said, 'that's better.'

'You'll be needing that,' she said.

'Too true,' I said. 'Too true.'

She smirked again. She sat there smirking for a long time. Then she uncrossed her legs so that I could see up her knickers. They were loose-legged and bright green with white lace. They looked knew. She watched me watch her. Slowly she got up, her arms still folded.

78

'Well,' she said, 'I'll let you get your rest.'

'Thanks,' I said.

She opened the door.

'Will you be going out tonight?' she said.

'Yes, probably,' I said.

'Because if you're back at a reasonable hour I'll do you some supper if you like.'

'That's very kind of you,' I said.

She didn't say anything and then she closed the door.

Six-thirty and Friday night. Too late for people going home from work and too early for people coming out to get drunk. Except for the workmen who were already in the pubs splashing their pay packets about.

I drove down the High Street. There was hardly any traffic. The remains of the sun were blustered into long shadows by the thin wind. I drove past Woolworth's and British Home Stores and Millet's and Willerby's. I drove past the Essoldo and the Pricerite and past the dead buildings at the end of town and abruptly I was out in the country. I followed the road as it rose up towards the top of the wolds. On either side of me, the steelworks darkened against the raggy, saffron sky. The road got steeper. I began to slow down, keeping to the crown, looking out on my right. There. There it was. I pulled the car over to the left and stopped and got out.

The air was not as noisy as I thought it would be. The wind was going. It was getting darker by the minute. I walked across the road. Just beyond the grass verge was a hedge and behind the hedge, hugging it, was an old rotten fence. There were tyre marks in the ground on the verge and there was a hole in the hedge and behind it I could only see a few splinters belonging to the fence. I went and stood in the hole in the hedge and looked down.

It was more of an incline than a drop. It stretched down for about a hundred and fifty feet until it came to the water that filled the bottom of the disused sandstone quarry. The quarry looked enormous but that was probably because of the hundreds of little islands of sandstone that rose above the water. They gave you the impression that they were bigger than they were because there was nothing to give them any scale, just the water. They were oblong shaped, twenty times as long as they were wide, with sloping sides forming ridges running the length of the islands. In the dusk it looked like a dumping ground for old Toblerone packets.

The car had been moved. From where I was there was nothing to show that it had ever been there. I turned slightly so I could look at the path the car had taken through the hedge. From the way it went, he'd been coming down hill, going towards town, which meant if it had been an accident, then he'd been drinking somewhere out of town in one of the villages – which was something else Frank wouldn't have done. If he'd got any drinking to do, drinking like that (which was something else) he wouldn't have left the town. As far as the outskirts, maybe, but not outside.

I walked back to the car and got in and sat there. I didn't really know why I'd come. Just to see, I suppose. Just to see what it looked like.

I drove off down the hill towards the town and as I drove I decided that tonight I had to spend in 'The Cecil'. I couldn't piss about. They knew I was in town anyway. All hanging about in 'The Cecil' would do would be to perhaps make them wonder why I hadn't gone home, make them think I knew something, make them decide that I hadn't just come for the funeral. And they'd know if Keith was tipping the wink. They'd see me and him and they'd get him and work on him until he told them things, which was hard luck for him but it would tell me what I wanted to know. He'd be able to put me on to the blokes who worked on him and from there I might get somewhere. Somewhere Gerald and Les wouldn't want me to get. I remembered what was said in Gerald's flat before I left. They'd both been there. Gerald in his county houndstooth and his lilac shirt, sitting at his Cintura topped desk, the picture window behind him. Belsize Park and Camden Town below him and Les sitting on the edge of the desk, in his corduroy suit, thumbing through a copy of *Punch*. I'd sat in the leather stud-backed chair with the round seat, and Audrey had poured the drinks and passed them round. She'd been wearing a culotte skirt and a ruffled blouse, a sort of Pop Paisley, and I'd wondered what would happen if Gerald found out that this time next week I'd be screwing her three thousand miles away instead of under his nose.

Gerald had said:

'I'm sure you're wrong, Jack. I can't really convince myself into seeing it your way. I'm sure it's the way it looks.'

'It smells shitty, Gerald. It's so strong it's blowing all the way down from the north into your air-conditioned system and right up my nose.'

'Well,' he'd said, 'if you feel you're right, feel it so strongly, what are you going to do?'

'I'm going to the funeral aren't I?'

'Yes, you are, and then what?'

'I'll see if anyone has any knowledge.'

'You'll start sniffing?'

'That's right.'

'Well, Jack, if Frank was mixed up, if he

82

was knocked off, then you can bet the coppers know all about it. And they're saying it was an accident. So if it wasn't, then they're keeping quiet because somebody with connections is involved.'

'That's probable.'

There'd been a silence.

'Of course,' Gerald had said, 'if that was the case, there are only two or three people up there who would have those kind of connections.'

'That's right.'

There was another silence.

'You know, of course, how much we value our business arrangements with a certain gentleman who lives in the vicinity of your home town?'

'Do me a favour.'

'Yes, right. Well, all I'm saying, Jack, is think. Whatever you come across, think. I wouldn't want the business, us, to be embarrassed in any way.'

'You don't know anything, do you, Gerald?'

'Jack...'

Another silence.

'All I can say is this,' he'd said. 'They'll all know you're there. That'll mean trouble. With some people, all right. With others, well ... we wouldn't want to make a bad situation worse by sticking by you. And if you caused a bit of trouble, and you got

sorted out, well, you wouldn't be all that fit
to do the job you're doing now. Would you?'

'I'll survive.'

'Of course you will, Jack. All I hope is you
won't do anything, you know, thoughtless.'

Les, still flicking through *Punch*, had said:

'One thing, Jack. If there has been any
funny business, and the scuffers are keeping
mum, well, if you create a bit more, they
might feel they'll have to do something. You
know. They don't like members from town
going up there and doing whatever they
like.'

'Yes,' said Gerald. 'It might get into the
papers, then they'd have to, like it or not.'

'I know all that,' I'd said, 'so don't tell me
about it.'

Another silence. Then Gerald had said:

'Well, there's only this; you do good work
for us, Jack. I'm not saying we couldn't do
without you, but it'd be an unnecessarily
difficult job finding someone to replace
you.'

I'd said nothing.

'So whichever way you look at things, have
a think before you make any important
decisions. Like going to a funeral, for
instance.'

He'd had to smile then, to make the last
bit seem like more of a joke than it was
meant to be.

I parked the car in 'The Cecil' car park,

84

but I didn't go in by the side door. I walked round the front and in by the main entrance.

I walked over to the bar. Keith was on duty three barmen away. He looked at me. I shook my head. He looked away. I had to keep up the pretence of secrecy in front of him in case he wondered why I wasn't bothering to play it cagey.

I got my drinks and turned round and leaned against the bar, so that I could see the Friday-nighters as they got them in down and over. Nothing had changed.

The double doors opened and a man came in.

He was fairly tall, on the thin side, his hair, what you could see of it, was dark, and he walked erect with one hand in his jacket pocket, royalty-style, a cigarette in his other hand, held at waist height, pressed into his middle, and he wore a peaked hat that had a very shiny visor and a double breasted blue serge suit, three-button, silver buttons, the kind of suit all chauffeurs wear.

It was my old friend Eric Paice. How nice to see him, I thought.

He walked up to the bar and pretended not to see me. He'd seen me the minute he'd opened the door, if not before.

While he was ordering I picked up my drinks and walked along to where he was standing. I gave him a minute while he counted out his change, still pretending.

'Hello, Eric.'

He turned. His expression was meant to be full of amazement. All that happened was his right eyebrow moved an eighth of an inch towards the peak of his cap.

'Good God,' he said.

I smiled.

'Jack Carter,' he said.

His voice was as surprised as his face.

'Eric,' I said. 'Eric Paice.'

He put his money in his pocket.

'You're the last person I should have expected to see round this way,' he said.

'Oh,' I said. 'You didn't know this is my home town, like?'

'Well, blow me,' he said. 'I never knew that.'

'Funny isn't it,' I said.

'So what're you doing? On your holidays?'

'Visiting relatives.'

'Relatives, eh? Very nice.'

'It would be. If they were still living.'

'How do you mean?'

'A bereavement. There's been a death in the family.'

'Oh, what a shame. Nothing serious, I hope.'

I gave him credit. His face was as straight as a poker.

'Yes,' I said. 'My brother. Car accident, you know.'

'Oh, dear,' he said. 'What a pity – here! Not that feller that went off top road? Monday?'

'That's right.'

'No! Well, blow me. Would you believe it. Read about it in paper, Tuesday night. And he was your brother, eh? Well, well. I mean, I read the name, but I never dreamt...'

'Small world,' I said.

He downed his drink.

'Are you having another?' I said.

He looked at his glass.

'Well,' he said, 'I shouldn't.'

I ordered more drinks. When they came I said: 'Fancy sitting down?'

'Well...' he said.

'Come on,' I said, 'we can talk about the old days.'

I walked over to one of the tables at the back. He made a show of deciding whether or not to follow. He followed me, as I knew he would.

I sat down and he sat down.

'Cheers,' I said.

He nodded, then drank. I looked at him.

He looked exactly the way he'd looked last time I'd seen him. Five years ago. In the office at the Hamburg Club off Praed Street, standing behind Jimmy the Welshman who'd been sitting behind his big antique desk, well, not his desk, the desk which Tony Pinner had provided him with, and Jimmy the Welshman had been sweating like the fat pig he was. Myself and Jock Mitchell and Ted Shucksmith had been standing at the other side of the desk. Jimmy the Welshman's sister, Eric's girl-friend, had been lying on the floor crying, which is what she'd been doing ever since Jock had put her there in order to stop her screaming. There had been no boys left to help Jimmy because since five minutes and three hundred pounds ago, three of them had started working for us and a fourth was lying in the toilet presently not working for anybody.

'You're out of a job, Jimmy,' I'd said to him. 'How's your pulling these days? You might have to brush up on it.'

He'd managed to say 'What's up?'

'Everything,' I'd said. 'This club isn't owned by Tony any more. Neither is the Matador, or the Manhatten or The Spinning Wheel. They are now owned by certain parties who have instructed me to inform you that as from tonight the gaff is under new management.'

He'd thought about that for a while. Then he'd sweated a bit more and he'd said:

'I can't leave. Tony'd kill me. You know what he'd do.'

I'd smiled at him.

'Get out, Jimmy,' I'd said. 'Tony doesn't care about you any more.'

He'd sat there for a bit and then very

quickly he'd got up from his desk almost knocking his chair over and he'd gone out. As he'd walked out, his sister had moaned at him but he'd stepped over her, not looking at her. After the door had closed, I'd said:

'That leaves you, Eric.'

'And the bird,' Jock'd said.

'What happened to the others?' Eric had asked.

'Seventy-five per cent are working for us.'

'And me?'

'Gerald still remembers Chiswick, Eric. He asked me to remind you about it.'

Eric's face had gone the colour of lemonade.

'Gerald's wife still has the marks, you know. I must admit they were very discreetly placed.'

'And Jack'd know,' Jock'd said, then he'd wished he hadn't because I'd looked at him.

'It was her,' Eric'd said, indicating the girl on the floor. 'It was her that wanted to do that. All I'd been told was to get hold of her and scare her, get Gerald rattled, you know. It was her that wanted to do that.'

'Of course, Eric. And just let's say that's the truth. You couldn't have stopped her, could you?'

'No,' he'd said, 'no, I couldn't. Wes the Spade was there. He egged her on. I couldn't do anything. Honest.'

'We were talking to Wes earlier,' I'd said.

'He said it was you two.'

'Ask Gerald's wife, then. Ask her. She'll tell you.'

'Audrey,' I'd said.

Audrey had walked into the office. Now Eric's face was ice-cream soda.

'What's the story, Audrey?'

Audrey had looked at the girl on the floor, who by then had been trying to crawl into the space under Jimmy's desk.

'Her,' she'd said. 'I want her.'

'Yes, I know,' I'd said. 'I know what you want. But the truth? Tell it to me. After all, if Gerald knew you were here...'

'I want her,' she'd said. 'He can watch. Unless he'd like to take her place.'

We'd all looked at Eric. He'd made no movement.

'So,' I'd said.

Audrey had sat on the edge of Jimmy's desk and had taken out a cigarette. Jock and Ted had picked up the girl and they'd neatly and quickly taken off her dress, put the belt to her dress on Jimmy's desk and tied her to Jimmy's chair.

'Eric,' the girl had said. 'Please.'

Eric had remained standing where he'd been when we'd first entered the office. Afterwards we'd let him walk out of the room and since then nobody had seen him around town. The way he'd looked when we'd let him go suggested he might have

90

been off for a long holiday.

And this was where he'd ended up. In a chauffeur's uniform in my home town. Acting quite normally towards me. Not afraid any more. Obviously working for someone. That's why I wasn't frightening him. He was at home. I was the away team. If he knew anything, had anything to do with it, and I hoped he had, he was cool; it didn't matter, he had his backers. He could afford not to shake. He could afford to drink with me. Oh Eric, I thought, I hope you can help me. I really do.

'Well, Eric,' I said. 'It's a small world isn't it?'

He nodded.

'Funny, too. Here I am, working in London, visiting my home town, and you, you're not living in your home town but working in mine.'

'Yeah, funny.'

'Who, er, who are you working for, Eric?'

He gave me a sidelong glance and smiled and snorted, which meant I must be out of my tiny mind.

I smiled too.

'I'm straight,' he said. 'Look at me. Respectable.'

'Come on,' I said. 'Who is it? It can only be one of three people.'

He carried on smiling into his beer and began shaking his head from side to side.

'Rayner?'

More smiling.

'Brumby?'

Shaking.

'Kinnear?'

Bigger smile than ever. He looked at me. I smiled back.

'Why do you care?'

'Me? I don't care, Eric. Just nosey.'

'That's not always a good way to be.'

I laughed and put my hand on his leg.

'So you're doing all right, Eric, then,' I said. 'You're making good.'

'Not bad.'

'Good prospects for advancement?'

He smiled again.

I squeezed his leg and smiled even bigger.

'All right, Eric,' I said. 'All right.'

I took a drink.

'When was the funeral?' he said.

'Today,' I said.

'Oh,' he said mildly, as if he didn't know. If he were here for a reason I hoped he was here for he'd know all right. He'd know what colour braces I'd worn to it.

'You'll be off back to town soon, then,' he said.

'Oh, pretty soon. Sunday or Monday. Got a bit of tidying up to do. Affairs. You know. Shouldn't be later than Monday.'

'Ah,' said Eric.

While we'd been talking the band had

92

drifted on to the stage. There was an old fat drummer in an old tux and a bloke on an electric bass and at the organ with all its magic attachments sat a baldheaded man with a shiny face, a blue crew neck sweater and a green cravat. They struck up with *I'm a Tiger.*

I got up.

'Off to the Gents,' I said. 'I'll be back in a minute.'

He nodded.

I picked my way through the noisy tables and went into the Gents. I stood in the anteroom and gave him a minute and then I opened a door on my left that led on to the car park.

It was blustering with rain again. Blue neon shone in puddles. Eric was standing by a Rolls Royce. He was looking towards the pub. He waited a few seconds then got into the car and started it up. I waited until he began to pull across the pavement into the main road. I ducked down and left the doorway and ran along a row of cars to where mine was. Meanwhile, Eric had turned left and pulled away, driving along the High Street towards the top end of the town.

I shot the car out of the parking space and across the tarmac to the exit on the other side of the car park, opposite the exit Eric had left by. The exit opened into Allenby

Street. It ran exactly parallel to the High Street. I turned right into Allenby Street.

I shot across three intersections without looking. I hadn't the time. I'd got sixty on the clock before I turned right again. In front of me, fifty yards away, was the High Street again, running across the top of the road. I reached the lights. They were at amber. I stopped. The High Street traffic began to slide across in front of me.

One of the last to cross was the Rolls.

The lights changed. I whipped round the corner. Eric was three cars in front. That was fine. I'd keep it like that.

I was very interested in where Eric might be going. If he'd come to 'The Cecil' to sound me out then he might be going to tell somebody about it and I'd like to know who. And then, he might have been told to show himself, to make me realise they knew I was there and they would do something about it if I made them, and if that was so, he still might be going to tell someone. Course, it might just have been an accident, bumping into me like that, but even then he'd know I was in town. Everybody would who mattered. And even the ones who mattered who hadn't had anything to do with Frank's killing would have a good idea of who did. And everything else apart, it would be very interesting to know who Eric was working for. Eric didn't love me very much, but the governor who employed him would love me even less, if only because I was a foreigner on the home turf. Frank or no Frank, they might feel happier if they were waving goodbye to me at the railway station.

At the top of the hill, where the High Street officially became City Road, Eric turned left. Here the road rose again, and wound upwards through the landscaped suburb that belonged to the town's wealthy. There were soft lawns and discreet trees and refined bushes and modern Georgian houses.

He turned left again, into a narrower road disappearing between banks of foliage. A sign at the turn-off said 'The Casino'. I drove past the entrance to give him time, then I turned and drove back and turned right. There was just enough room for two cars to get by one another. Then the trees stopped. There was a gravel car park and a lot of cars. Beyond the car park was 'The Casino'. It looked like the alternative plan to the new version of Euston Station. White low and ugly. A lot of glass. A single piece of second storey that was a penthouse. A lot of sodium lighting. Plenty of phoney ranch-house brickwork. Probably the worst beer for seventy miles.

The Rolls was parked in a reserved space.

I parked my car and walked over to the glassy entrance. There was a doorman in

Tom Arnold livery. I walked past him and into the huge foyer. There were only two bouncers. One at either end, like book-ends. They both took me in but allowed me to get as far as the reception desk. The man behind the desk looked as though he'd graduated from Bingo calling. In his younger days he might have crooned in provincial palais.

'Good evening, sir,' he said, his quiff bobbing. 'Are you a member?'

'I don't know,' I said.

I leant on the desk, using one arm, hand clenched. I unclenched the hand and kept the fingers suspended so that he could see the money. Somehow he managed to look past me at the bouncers without taking his eyes off my face. He was thinking very seriously. He chanced it with the bouncers.

He took the money and as he picked it up a small pink card took its place on the desk top.

'Yes,' he said, loud enough for the bouncers to hear, 'that's right, sir. Mr Jackson's guest. He's signed you in and is waiting for you inside. Would you sign in too please?'

I signed my real name and picked up the pink card. I drifted away from the desk and down the steps towards the door that led into the first gambling rooms. I flashed my card at a third bouncer who was standing by the door and who looked at me as though he didn't like me very much.

As I walked through the door one of the two book-end bouncers began to saunter over to the reception desk.

Inside, the décor was pure British B-feature except with better lighting.

The clientele thought they were select. There were farmers, garage proprietors, owners of chains of cafés, electrical contractors, builders, quarry owners; the new Gentry. And occasionally, though never with them, their terrible offspring. The Sprite drivers with the accents not quite right, but ten times more like it than their parents, with their suède boots and their houndstooth jackets and their ex-grammar school girl-friends from the semi-detached trying for the accent, indulging in a bit of finger pie on Saturday after the halves of pressure beer at the 'Old Black Swan', in the hope that the finger pie will accelerate the dreams of the Rover for him and the mini for her and the modern bungalow, a farmhouse style place, not too far from the Leeds Motorway for the Friday shopping.

I looked around the room and saw the wives of the new Gentry. Not one of them was not overdressed. Not one of them looked as though they were not sick to their stomachs with jealousy of someone or something. They'd had nothing when they were younger, since the war they'd gradually got the lot, and the change had been so surprising they could never stop wanting, never be satisfied. They were the kind of people who made me know I was right.

But while all these thoughts were making me feel the way I always feel I noticed that the bouncer who had gone over to the reception desk had come through the door and was trying to see where I was, so I stepped behind a square white-gloss pillar (it was that kind of place) and looked at him from behind some thin wrought-iron trellis-work (it was also that kind of place). He looked sick because naturally he couldn't see me, so he pulled his jacket more squarely on his shoulders, which was the equivalent to him swallowing a lump in his throat, and made for a place where there was somebody he could tell all about it. There was one of those doors that lead somewhere and he went through it. I wended my weary way across the room and opened the door. In front of me was a flight of juicily carpeted stairs. On either side of me were two doors like the one I'd just closed behind me. Somewhere above me I could hear voices. I went up the stairs, turned sharp right and there were another eight stairs. Beyond these eight stairs was a short landing and an open doorway. From my position at the turn I could see the back of the bouncer's D.J.

'Well, he must be somewhere downstairs, I suppose,' the bouncer was saying.

'You stupid fucker,' a voice from the room beyond said.

Good old Eric.

'Well, I didn't know,' said the bouncer.

'No,' said a different voice, honed on about two million cigarettes, 'and you never will, I don't suppose.'

The bouncer continued holding the door open.

'Well?' said the second voice. 'Hadn't you better go and see what he's doing?'

The bouncer jumped back to life, but not half as much as he jumped when he turned and saw me gazing into his eyes from about six inches away. He didn't exactly scream but his blow-wave went for a burton. I blew him a kiss and walked past him into the penthouse room.

It was all glass with black night and crayon neon beyond. The carpet lapped at the glass all the way round the room. There seemed to be a lot of low tables and little white rugs. Now the trick with this room was you'd think with all that glass about you'd be able to see what was going on from outside any time of day or night. But they'd been very clever and amusing and witty and they'd made most of the room five feet below floor level. So what you'd got was a room with a gallery of six feet going all the way round this enormous area that housed all these soft leather sofas and soft leather chairs and Swedish lamps and a roulette wheel set in a very beautiful antique rosewood table, a nicely appointed little bar, a very nice and spacious table which was for some reason or another covered with green baize. They'd had a very nice thought for decorating this green baize; they'd arranged little groups of cards with patterned backs to lay adjacent to slightly less neat, rather more ostentatious piles of money. Around the table, on chairs, there were men. Another man was standing up behind a chair on which one of the other men was sitting. They were all looking up at me, as were the three girls who were arranged variously on the soft leather sofas and the soft leather chairs.

I walked over to the edge of the drop and leant on a padded rail. The man with the voice like two million cigarettes raised his eyebrows and said slowly and petulantly:

'You see what it's like, these days, Jack,' he said. 'You can't get the material.' I sensed the bouncer's embarrassment behind me. 'How can you run anything when that's the kind of material you get.'

He inhaled and exhaled. 'I could weep. I really could. I sometimes think I'll retire. Just get out and piss off to Ibiza or somewhere and then let them try and find somebody else to employ them. If I wasn't so philanthropic they'd be down at the Labour standing behind the coons.' Inhale, exhale and a wave of the hand. 'Do you get this, Jack? Is it the same in the smoke? I expect it is. Everything's going down the nick. Except for blokes like you and Eric, but then you're like me. You've had the hard times harden you. Not like these cunts. Getting tough is practising fifty breaks at snooker and reading Hank Janson. I sometimes wish I had a time machine. I'd take 'em back and show 'em me at their age. Then I'd leave 'em there and tell them to get in touch with me when they catch up to nineteen-seventy and let me know how they made out. But I'd never know though. They'd never catch up.'

The bouncer was still there sending out waves like oil fired central heating.

'Clear off, Ray,' said the man, 'and pay off Hughie. Give him his money, less what Jack gave him, and this time close the door behind you.' The door closed behind him.

The man looked at Eric who was looking at me. The man smiled and looked at me too.

'Never mind, Eric,' he said. 'Nobody's perfect. You should have caught a bus instead.'

Cyril Kinnear was very, very fat. He was the kind of man that fat men like to stand next to. He had no hair and a handlebar moustache that his face made look a foot long on each side. In one way it was a very pleasant face, the face of a wealthy farmer or of an ex-Indian army officer in the used car business but the trouble was he had eyes like a ferret's. They had black pupils an eighth of an inch in diameter surrounded by whites the colour of the fish part of fish fingers.

He was also only five foot two inches tall.

'Hello, Mr Kinnear,' I said.

'Well, don't just stand there,' he said. 'Come and join us.' He laughed. *'Come and join us, come and join us, we're the soldiers of the Lord,'* he sang. 'Joy, get Jack a drink. What is it, Jack, scotch? Get Jack a scotch.'

I walked down the cedarwood planked stairs.

Of the other three men round the table, one was slim and elegant with distinguished grey flecks in his wind-tunnel-tested toupée, another looked as though the trousers to his dinner suit should be tucked into gumboots, and the third was just a little rat with a tiny permanently frightened rat's face.

'Jack, sit down,' said Kinnear.

I sat down on a sofa next to the best looking of the birds. She was a long-haired blonde, more thin than fat, with a face that ten years ago would have got her somewhere in the modelling business (I mean the advertising one) or maybe a film part opposite Norman Wisdom, but even if those things had still been open to her in nineteen-seventy, she had today's look that told me she wouldn't have bothered. She smiled into her drink as I sat down, then smiled at me and then smiled into her drink again.

The girl called Joy brought me my drink. She was strictly Harrison Marks.

'Ta,' I said. 'Cheers, Mr Kinnear.'

'Cheers, Jack,' he said. 'All the best.' Kinnear and I drank. The others kept on looking.

'I hope I'm not interrupting anything,' I said.

'Of course not, Jack,' said Kinnear. 'I hope I didn't give you that impression because of that little business with Ray. It's just that I pay him to know things. You know.'

'Gerald and Les asked me to call and give you their regards,' I said. 'Seeing as I was coming up anyway.'

'Nice thought,' said Kinnear. 'Nice boys. How are they? How's business?'

'Pretty good.'

'Of course it is. Of course it is.'

A silence.

'Eric told me about your bereavement.'

'Yes,' I said.

'Do you know, I never knew he worked for

103

me. I never knew your brother worked for me.'

'Funny,' I said.

'If I'd have known, well, I would have fixed him up somehow.'

'Yes,' I said.

'Nasty way to go,' said Kinnear, 'a car crash – Joy, Joy, look give Jack another drink, no, give him the bloody bottle, that's better, you can't offer a man like Jack drinks in pissing little glasses like that.'

I was given the bottle. The girl sitting next to me looked at the neck as I held it upright and giggled. She was drunk.

The man with the gum-boot manner spoke: 'Are we here to play cards or are we here to talk about the good old days?'

Kinnear shifted his weight in his chair and gaped at the speaker.

'Harry,' he said. 'Harry. Of course we are. Of course – Jack. I'm sorry, I don't want to be rude, but these gentlemen have brought a lot of money with them – hang on, hang about – perhaps you'd like a hand? A couple of rounds? Take your mind off things? You lads don't mind? The more the merrier eh? Eric, get Jack a chair, will you?'

'No, I won't just now thanks, Mr Kinnear,' I said. 'I have to be going soon.'

'Well, you just do as you please. Make yourself comfortable while we carry on.'

'Thanks,' I said.

The man with the greying wig began to deal. Kinnear's eyes were as black as liquorice. Eric looked as though he wanted to spit at me. I relaxed on the sofa and watched Kinnear. He didn't like it. He never looked at me, but I knew, and he knew that I knew. He didn't like anything very much at the moment, from the way I'd got in to the way I was sitting, but he was forced to give me this old pals routine not because he wanted to save face in front of his mateys but because I knew he was narked. It was the only way for him to be. But whether he was narked because a London boy had made his chauffeur look daft and his boys look dafter, or whether he was narked for other reasons, I didn't know.

The girl sitting next to me said: 'You know Les Fletcher, do you?'

'I work for him.'

'Do you?'

'Yes, I do.'

She smiled her private oh-so-clever-oh-so-knowing-but-oh-isn't-everything-a-drag smile. It made her look very simple as well as very drunk. I thought the conversation had ended until she spoke again.

'I know him too,' she said.

'Oh, do you?'

'Yes.'

'No,' I said, 'do you really?'

'Yes,' she said. 'I met him last year.'

'Go on,' I said in a fascinated voice.

'Oh yes. When he came up on business.'

'Really?'

'Yes. He came to see Mr Kinnear.'

'No.'

'Oh yes. We went about together.'

'Yes?'

'Yes, while he was here.'

'While he was here?'

'He was here for four days. About.'

I shook my head as though I could hardly believe what she'd just said. She went back to looking in her glass.

'I'll open,' said the gum-boots man. 'Give me two.'

Grey Wig gave him two cards. The Rat was next. He stared at his hand for about twenty-four hours and said: 'I'll take four.'

'Three now, one later,' said Grey Wig as he dealt them.

Grey Wig himself took three. Kinnear fondled his moustache.

'Oh, I don't know,' he said. 'What shall I do? What shall I do? Oh – I think I'll stay as I am.'

Rat Face look up sharply and Grey Wig gave a thin smile.

Gum Boots said: 'Bloody bluffing bastard.'

'That's what you pay to find out,' said Kinnear. 'Isn't that right, Jack?'

'That's right,' I said. 'If you can afford it.'

'I thought you said you were going soon,' said Gum Boots.

'Soon,' I said. 'After you've lost your money, which won't be very long.'

Gum Boots looked at me for a long time. 'Clever sod, aren't you?' he said.

'Comparatively,' I said, giving him his look back.

Gum Boots was about to say something back when Kinnear spoke.

'Harry,' he said, 'I don't like to push, but could you let us know how much your hand's worth?'

Gum Boots gave off looking at me for a minute and pushed a tenner into the middle. He was about to look back at me when Rat Face captured his attention by stacking.

'Christ Almighty,' said Gum Boots. 'Not again.'

Rat Face fidgeted. 'Well...' he said.

'Every bloody time,' said Gum Boots. 'Every bloody time he stacks. He only goes if he's got higher than a full house. Why the bloody hell do you ask him to play, Cyril?'

'Harry,' said Kinnear, 'however he plays, he certainly doesn't lose the way you do.'

Gum Boots went black. Grey Wig pushed a tenner in. They all went round a couple of times pushing tenners until Kinnear said:

'Well, I don't know. Let's see how we all feel. I'll follow the ten and I'll raise it to fifty.'

'What's that? Fifty?' said Gum Boots.

'That's right, Harry,' said Kinnear.

Gum Boots sorted out fifty and pushed it in. Grey Wig smiled to himself and did the same. Kinnear pushed in another fifty, then with studied staginess counted out another fifty.

'What's that?' said Gum Boots.

'That, Harry? That's another fifty pounds – ten five pound notes of the realm.'

'Hundred altogether?'

'A hundred altogether, Harry.'

Gum Boots looked at the money and then at his cards which were face down on the table. He was dying to pick up the cards to have another look to reassure him of their strength. He managed to contain himself and somehow he got the hundred into the middle without shredding the notes into little pieces.

Grey Wig gave the classic smile and shake of the head and turned in his cards. Kinnear picked up his cards and pursed his lips and sucked in his breath and looked at his hand. Gum Boots managed not to drum his fingers on the edge of the table. Kinnear finally stopped playing and said:

'I'll follow that and go another hundred.'

Gum Boots looked very sick.

'You could always see me, Harry,' said Kinnear.

Gum Boots was staring at Kinnear's hand

as if he was trying to burn his way through to the other side. He had the choice of putting in another two hundred and seeing what Kinnear had got or he could put in another two hundred without seeing Kinnear in the hope that Kinnear would fold at the sight of Gum Boots following. It all depended on whether or not Kinnear was bluffing. Gum Boots had to make a decision. A decision based on the one hundred and eighty pounds of his that was already in the kitty.

He must have decided that Kinnear was bluffing.

'All right,' he said, his voice like water gurgling down a plughole. 'Two hundred.'

He pushed the two hundred pounds into the middle.

Kinnear raised his eyebrows slightly.

'Mm!' he said.

Then he got up and went over to a cupboard and unlocked it and took some money out of it. He sat down again and counted out a lot of notes. He put the notes in the kitty.

'What's that?' said Gum Boots.

'That's six hundred pounds, Harry,' said Kinnear. 'Two hundred to follow you and I've raised it to four hundred.'

'Four hundred,' said Gum Boots.

'That's right,' said Kinnear.

'You're not seeing me,' said Gum Boots.

'No, Harry,' said Kinnear.

Gum Boots would have swallowed if he could have stopped his Adam's apple from rushing up and down his neck. Now he was back to where he was a few minutes ago. Except now it was four hundred to play the game. Gum Boots must have still thought Kinnear was bluffing, but he didn't want to go to eight hundred next time round. So he saw him.

He reached down by the side of his chair and picked up a briefcase. He took out a lot of money and counted some of it out and put it in the middle of the table.

'I'll see you,' he said.

'Calling my bluff, are you, Harry?' Kinnear smiled at him.

Gum Boots nodded.

'Well now,' said Kinnear, 'let's see what I've got. I've forgotten what I had with all the excitement. Oh yes. I expect it's yours, Harry.'

Kinnear laid his hand down. He had a hearts flush, Queen high.

Gum Boots turned the colour of a piece of very old Camembert.

'Oh come on, Harry,' said Kinnear, 'I haven't won, have I? Go on, you're pulling my leg.'

Kinnear reached across the table to turn over Gum Boots cards but Gum Boots grabbed them first and stacked them with the pack. Kinnear laughed.

'How about that, eh, Jack?' he said. 'Old Harry thought I was having him on.'

'You've got to be a good poker player to play poker with a good poker player,' I said.

'Shut up,' said Gum Boots.

Kinnear laughed again. I stood up.

'Not going are you, Jack?' said Kinnear.

'Have to,' I said. 'Things to see to.'

'Of course, of course,' he said. 'Well, any time you've a bit more time, drop in again. Like to see you.'

'I will do,' I said. 'If I can fit it in,'

The girl on the sofa giggled.

'Give my regards to Gerald and Les,' said Kinnear.

'I'll do that,' I said. I walked up the stairs and over to the door. The silence was hard and pure. I opened the door and it made a very loud noise as it ruffled the fitted carpet. Everybody was looking at me. I smiled across at Gum Boots.

'I told you I wouldn't be staying long,' I said.

Gum Boots swore.

I went out.

I'd got downstairs as far as the door that I'd come in through when I heard the upstairs door go. I waited. Eric appeared on the stairs. He walked down and joined me. I put my hand on the door knob and looked at him. His eyes were full of not very friendly thoughts.

'I didn't like that very much, Jack,' he said.

I smiled at him.

'If you'd have told me who you were working for it wouldn't have happened,' I said.

'Cyril didn't like it either.'

'Cyril, eh?' I said. 'All girls together is it?'

'But you've not been as clever as you think you have. You've got Cyril thinking. Like you got me thinking. He's wondering why you wanted to know who I work for.'

'Doesn't he know?'

'No, he bloody doesn't. But maybe he's thinking that Gerald and Les might like to know you're sticking your nose in. He gets the idea they wouldn't like that very much.'

'He's right. So tell him to save the money on the phone call.'

'You see,' he said, 'Cyril wonders why you should go to the trouble of playing cops and robbers just to find out who I worked for.'

'I told him,' I said. 'Gerald and Les asked me to give him their regards. I'd been told where to find him. Following you was incidental.'

I grinned at the way Eric looked at me. Then he turned away and started to walk back up the stairs.

'Tell Kinnear I'll be leaving as soon as I've cleared up Frank's affairs,' I said.

Eric turned round and looked at me.
'Goodnight, Eric,' I said.

I drove down the narrow road that led away
from 'The Casino'. The dark, close trees
came to an end and I was back bathing in
the rateable value of the yellow street lights.
There was nobody about. The California-
style houses were still and silent, tucked
away beyond the yards and yards of civic
style lawn. Where a house showed signs of
life naturally the curtains were drawn well
back to inform the neighbours of the riches
smugly placed within. Well placed conifers
stood sentry over the suburb's snug and
wealthy taxpayers.

I remembered this place when it was
called Back Hill.

Back Hill. The woods used to seem to
stretch up to the sky. Except for the patches
of red-brown earth that showed through
here and there. You could see the hill from
the end of Jackson Street. And although the
hill was a natural place for kids to play, there
were never very many kids up there when
Frank and I used to roam about. We used to
go up there on a Saturday morning and it
seemed as though we'd wander for bloody
miles. There were all kinds of secret places
that were Frank's and my private property.
When we were older, getting on for sixteen,
we'd stroll about taking turns carrying the

shotgun, placing it in the crook of the arm, just so, like cowboys, Wellingtons making that good slopping sound, lumberjacket collars turned up, taking things slow, occasionally stopping in a hidden hollow, squatting down on our haunches, just looking around, cold breath curling up to the grey sky, not talking, feeling just right. Of course that was before I met Albert Swift. Before the fight between me and my dad. Before the driving. Before Ansley School. Before a lot of things. But it used to be a great place to be. You could walk to the top (and there was a top, a small flat plateau covered in grass that whipped about in the wind) and you wouldn't turn round until you got to this plateau and then you'd look down and over the tops of the trees and you'd see the town lying there, just as though it had been chucked down in handfuls: the ring of steelworks, the wolds ten miles away to the right rising up from the river plain, the river itself eight miles away dead ahead, a gleaming broadness, and more wolds, even higher, receding beyond it. And above it all, the broad sky, wider than any other sky could be, soaring and sweeping, pushed along by the north winds.

This place, the plateau, was where we'd spend most of our time on Back Hill. In March, we'd huddle under the one bush that grew right on the edge, and we'd be just below the edge, on a sandy ridge, out of the wind, and we'd watch the March wind beat-up the white horses on the river. In August, we'd lie on our backs and look up at the blue sky with its pink flecks on our eyes and a tall blade of grass would occasionally incline into my vision and Frank would talk really more to himself than to me about what he liked and what he'd like to do. Jack, he'd say, those seventy-eights I got yesterday in Arcade, don't you reckon that that one by the Benny Goodman Sextet *Don't Be That Way*, was the best? That drumming by Gene Krupa. Hell! Wouldn't it be great to be able to do that? But if you could, you couldn't do it in this hole. Nobody's interested. They'd say it was a row. You can do things like that in America. They encourage you because they think jazz is dead good. America. That'd be the place, though, wouldn't it? Imagine. Those cars with all those springs that rock back and forwards like a see-saw when you put the brakes on. You can drive one of them when you're sixteen over there. Just think, our kid. Driving one of those along one of them highways wearing a drape suit with no tie, like Richard Widmark, with the radio on real loud listening to Benny Goodman. Cor! I reckon when I leave school I'll go to America. Work my passage. I could easy get a job. Even labourers out there get fifty quid a week. Electricians and

115

that can get two hundred. They can. And you can go to pictures at two in morning and see three pictures in one programme. You could get one of them houses with big lawns and no fences.

I drove down the hill past the houses with the big lawns and no fences.

'The Cecil'. I parked the car again and went in. The lights were lower now. A crooner in a John Collier suit was trying to sound like Vince Hill. I went over to the bar and ordered a large scotch. Keith was serving at the far end of the bar. The bar was three deep in blokes. The tables had at least six people round each one. The crooner finished. A lot of people clapped and whistled. The crooner turned into his M.C. bit and said:

'And now, Ladies and Gentlemen, and especially gentlemen, I'd like to introduce the star attraction for tonight, a little lady who's no stranger to these parts, someone who's having a highly successful tour of the northern clubs, and who's managed for one night and one night only to squeeze (and I mean squeeze) in an appearance here for us tonight. In fact she needs no introduction from me, Ladies and Gentlemen, may I present Miss ... Jackie ... Du ... Val!'

Loud cheers and whistles and all the blokes at the bar shoved along to get nearer

116

to the front. The music started. *Big Spender.*
Miss Jackie Du Val walked on to the stage,
arms raised high. She was wearing a
tangerine evening gown and matching
gloves that didn't. She had black hair wound
up into a grotesque bee-hive and if she was
this side of forty she was only just. She
walked along the short dais that led a bit of
the way into the tables and the band got
round to the beginning of the tune again
and she began to sing à la Bassey, only
louder. As she sang she began going into the
routine of first one glove and then the next
and pushing the fishnet knee through the
slit in her dress and I thought Jesus Christ!
and turned to the bar and looked at the
bottles and read the labels.

After I'd done that I thought about me
and Audrey. And like when I usually
thought about me and Audrey it was with
mixed feelings: I used to think, Christ, what
a bloody idiot thing to do, start shacking up
with the boss's wife when you're on such a
good number and then I used to think
about the things Audrey could do to make
me act like a bloody idiot.

God, she was good.

I'd never had anyone like her. Not that I'd
had a lot. I'd had it regular from the slags
that worked for us, but the trouble was all
I'd had to do was to phone up and a couple
of them'd be round in half an hour. And

117

more than likely gone in half an hour.

But when Audrey touched me for the first time, that's what it was like: the first time, and it'd taken me all my time not to blow it as soon as her fingers'd felt me.

But she'd made me wait and that'd had something to do with it too.

She'd only been married to Gerald for eight months before I started getting the picture. Gerald'd picked her up out in Viareggio while he'd been on his holidays. He'd come back early and given Rae and their two kids the boot and he'd moved Audrey in straight away. They'd got married the day the divorce came through. Les'd thought Gerald'd been a bit of a cunt about it all but he'd never told Gerald to his face. Gerald'd been like a bloody kid over her. Everything she wanted she got. But it wasn't because of Gerald she'd got me. She'd managed that all by herself.

Keith wandered up. He was polishing a glass. He could afford the time while they were all gawping.

'Hello Keith,' I said.

'Somebody been asking about you,' he said.

'Oh, yes?' I said. 'Anybody we know?'

'Remember we were talking about Thorpey? The loan merchant?'

'Old Thorpey, eh? Haven't seen him in a long time.'

'That's what he was saying about you.'

'Oh, yes?'

'Yes. He said he'd heard you were visiting town and he was wondering if I knew where you were staying at, like. Wanted to look you up. Old times' sake and that.'

'That's nice of him.'

'I would have come to tell you but I didn't think you'd be there.'

'Sure.'

Keith began to go red.

'I would have come, honest.'

'What did you tell him?'

He went redder.

'Nowt,' he said.

'Good. How was it left?'

'They went after they realised I wasn't letting on.'

'They?'

'There were three of them.'

I lit a fag.

'Thorpey, eh?'

Thorpey was the kind of rat who I would have thought preferred to work on his own. Not for a governor, at any rate. He'd always been very full of himself. He'd liked being a top dog in his own little way, and the business he operated saw him very nicely. He'd like the profit margin kept the way it was. Supposing Frank had done something to upset Thorpey? Which of course he wouldn't. But supposing. What could Frank have done to

Thorpey that warranted Thorpey going to the trouble of knocking Frank off? Even if Thorpey and his lads had half the nerve. So if Thorpey was on his own, there'd be no need for him to want to see me. But, of course, there might have been a merger. The loan systems in Doncaster and Bradford and Leeds and Barnsley and Grimsby all owned by one governor might have been added to by seconding Thorpey's little operation, just to make things nice. Thorpey would still be the figurehead, but from time to time whoever he was working for would ask him to do this and that, things that on his own Thorpey normally would have steered clear of. Like having a little talk with me. Or filling Frank up with scotch and letting the hand brake off his car.

I looked at the clock on the wall. It was quarter to ten.

'You wouldn't happen to know where they went?' I said.

Keith shrugged.

'Could have gone anywhere. The clubs, pubs, anywhere. But wherever they are, they'll be looking for you.'

I didn't say anything.

'What are you off to do?' asked Keith.

'Go and see somebody who can give me a little bit of gossip.'

'Who?'

'Oh, just an old friend I haven't seen in

years,' I said.

I walked away from the bar. Miss Jackie Du Val was naked except for a g-string. She'd come off the stage and now she was moving between the tables. There was hands all over the place. One bloke held up a pint of mild and Miss Jackie Du Val sat down on his knee and dipped her left breast in it. There was a load of laughter until the woman who was with the bloke with the pint of mild grabbed it and chucked it all over Miss Jackie Du Val and the bloke. The bloke got up and Miss Jackie Du Val hit the floor shrieking. The bloke socked the woman he was with and began wiping himself down. The woman fell over a chair and landed on the floor too. She and Miss Jackie Du Val found each other and began rolling about on the floor pulling and scratching and biting. There was much cheering. The woman on top of Miss Jackie Du Val was trying to bite one of Miss Jackie Du Val's titties while Miss Jackie Du Val was trying to remove both of the woman's eyes. A very drunken woman on the edge of the circle the crowd was making round them put her foot forward and with the toe of her shoe lifted the dress of the woman on top right up to her waist. There was more shrieking laughter. A couple of barmen had vaulted the bar and were trying to get through the crowd. The bloke who'd had the mild all over him stopped wiping himself and picked up a pint bottle of brown ale and emptied it slowly and deliberately over the upturned bottom of the woman on top, moving the bottle from side to side so that the woman's pants were evenly soaked. The woman began to screech her rage as I went through the doors and out into the High Street.

There's a place on the edge of town where they'd built a council estate somewhere back in the fifties. This place used to be what you could call a natural piece of waste land. What I mean is, there'd never been anything there that had been knocked down or carted away (like an old aerodrome) to give it that used look, laid waste, the kind of land where those erect and rusty weeds grow upright between old half-bricks and cracks in grey concrete; they just grew here anyway. The place used to stretch for the best part of a quarter of a mile away from the town. In another town they would have turned it into allotments. But in another town it might have looked as if something could be grown there.

Before they built the estate there, there had been only one house near this place, right on the very edge, as far away from the town as it could be. It was a symmetrical double-fronted Victorian farmhouse. The

122

colour of the bricks wasn't quite red. The window frames had been painted lime green approximately seventy-four years ago. Now, although there were curtains at the windows you couldn't see them from the outside. The chimney was in the middle of the roof and whether it was December or July it was always smoking. There was a shed at the back, about forty yards away from the house, and two hundred yards beyond this, the steelworks began, black at first, then glowing into savage flames.

There was no formal garden to the house, no garden fence. The weeds just got shorter the closer you got to the house. If you wanted to drive up to the house you bumped the car off the road over the grass verge and just took the straightest line between two points. Which was what I did.

I stopped the car and got out. There was the occasional clank and groan from the formless black and gold of the steelworks. The wind droned across my face. I walked towards the house. There were no lights on at the front. I went round the back. A motorbike and sidecar was illuminated by light from the naked bulb inside the kitchen. I knocked on the door. A woman of around seventy opened it. She stepped back to let me in and said:

'You'll have to wait a few moments, she's engaged at present.'

Stepping through I said: 'I've come to see Albert.'

'Oh,' she said and began to close the door. 'Albert, there's a feller to see you. What shall I say?'

But before she was able to close the door I was inside the kitchen.

The telly was in the corner. It was turned up full blast. Sitting on a high stool to one side of the telly with her back to me was a woman in a top-coat with her hair in curlers. She was sitting hunched up with her hands in her coat pockets. She didn't turn round but carried on looking at the telly. Two kids, about five or six years old, girls, were sitting on the floor watching telly as well. One of them turned her head round and looked at me for a minute then looked back at the screen. Her face was as filthy as her clothes. On the kitchen table amongst the dirty plates from at least half a dozen meals was a carry-cot. Inside the carry-cot was a baby that was no more than two months old.

Across on the other side of the table, near the wall next to a teak cocktail cabinet that was the only new piece of furniture in the room was a chair also facing the telly and in the chair sat a man with a glass in his hand who was looking at me with some surprise.

'Hello, Albert,' I said.

'Christ,' said Albert Swift, 'Jack Carter.'

The last time I'd seen him was eleven years ago after I'd come out the wrong side of eighteen months. I'd gone to see him to get my old job back but eighteen months had been a long time. They'd got a new driver and Albert had liked him very much because he hadn't any form. Albert had been very sympathetic but sympathy didn't go very far. So for three years I'd worked on my own. Until I'd decided to move to the smoke. But there'd been no hard feelings between me and Albert. In fact he'd let me have a few bob to see me clear. We'd known each other too long for hard feelings.

I'd met him when I was fifteen. He was three years older than me. He'd got a gang in Mortimer Street. A right tearaway was Albert. The first real tearaway I'd met. Me and Frank had been playing billiards at the Liberal club, a big chapel-like building on Kenworthy Road. There used to be two snooker tables and a table-tennis table and as many Dandelion and Burdocks as you could get down you. Only us kids used the place in the week. An old twat called Waller Havercroft looked after it. During the day he worked on the Dilly Cart and by Christ he hated us kids. Especially me. Anyway, me and Frank were playing billiards on the far table at the gloomiest end of the hall, and there was just the billiard light on and the light from Waller's office at the other end and it was really snug, the green cloth had that silent cosiness and we were really enjoying ourselves, saying nowt, taking our time, watching the nice straight angles the billiard balls were tracing on the table. Then the door'd burst open and Albert Swift and his gang had walked in. Albert'd been wearing a wide-boy's jacket, double breasted with padding all over the place, tartan shirt and brown corduroy trousers. He'd looked round the place and said, 'Jesus'. One of his gang'd spat on the floor. Old Waller'd been going to come out of his office and shoot them out until he'd seen who it was. He'd got a bit of the way out of his room and then he'd tried to get back in again without them noticing. But they did. Albert had turned to Waller and very sarcastically had said:

'Oh yes?'

Waller, still retreating, turning away to go back into his room, had mumbled something about something or other.

'D'you what?' Albert'd said. Waller'd closed the half-door with the little ledge on top that you used to put the money on for your Dandelion and Burdock.

'Did you say something, Old Cock?' Albert'd said.

Waller'd shot the bolt and lowered his eyes. Albert had taken out a cig and put it in his mouth and lit it and kept the match going then he'd taken a penny banger from his top pocket and lit the blue touch paper.

'I say, Old Cock. Were you saying something to me?' he'd said.

Waller'd retreated farther back into his office, but there hadn't been all that much farther for him to go. The banger'd started zizzing furiously. Albert'd flicked the banger over the top of the half-door. Waller'd almost fallen over a crate of pop bottles trying to get out of the way. The banger had boomed. Waller had shrieked. Albert's boys had laughed. One of them had taken another banger out and lit it and he'd tossed it in the office as well. Frank and me had stopped playing billiards the minute they'd come through the door. We'd been the only two kids in the place. Albert'd taken another banger from his top pocket. Frank'd put down his billiard cue and moved to the end of the table that was nearest the gang.

'I don't think you ought to do that,' he'd said.

Albert'd turned to face him.

'And who the fuckin' hell are you?'

Frank hadn't answered.

'Eh?' Albert'd said.

Albert and the gang had walked over and stood in front of Frank.

'You could hurt somebody,' Frank'd said.

'Did anybody ask you, cunt?' Albert'd said.

Frank hadn't answered. Albert'd leaned

forward and patted Frank's face and ruffled his hair.

'Think you're clever, do you?' Albert'd said.

Frank hadn't moved. He'd just stood there not saying anything. Albert'd pushed Frank so that Frank had to steady himself on the edge of the snooker table.

'Come on, then,' Albert'd said. 'Are you off to do something about it?'

'I don't fight,' Frank'd said.

'What do you do then?' Albert'd said. 'Smack handies?'

They'd all laughed.

Albert'd lit the banger he'd taken out and offered it to Frank. Frank wouldn't take it. Albert'd held the firework against Frank's pullover and Frank'd tried to wriggle away from Albert but Albert had got him pinned against the snooker table. Just before the banger was due to go off Albert'd stuffed it down Frank's pullover and jumped back. Frank'd managed to shake his pullover in time and the banger hadn't exploded until it was about a foot from the floor in its fall from Frank's pullover. Frank'd jumped up in the air to try to get out of the way. They'd all laughed. Frank'd pulled himself together and he'd walked back to where his cue had been and picked it up.

'Your shot, our kid,' he'd said, his voice shaking.

I'd felt sick. At that moment I'd hated Frank. I could have killed him. I'd lost everything I'd ever felt for him. He'd shown himself up. He hadn't wanted to fight. He'd let Albert scare him by not doing anything. I'd felt like crying. I'd stared at him for a long time after he'd spoken.

Then Albert had begun walking round the corner of the table to where Frank was so I'd made the shot but I hit it as hard as I could so that the red flew off the table and just missed Albert. Albert'd stopped and looked at me. I'd straightened up and stared back.

'Sorry,' I'd said. 'Me cue slipped.'

Albert'd carried on looking at me.

'Want to make owt of it?' I'd said.

'Jack,' Frank'd said.

'Fuck off,' I'd said. Then to Albert: 'Come on then. Or are you frit?'

Albert'd bellowed with laughter.

'I eat four of you every day for breakfast,' he'd said.

I'd thrown my cue down and I'd run round the table to get at Albert but Frank had got to me first and he'd managed to hold me back.

'Your bloody kid's got more spunk than you'll ever have, cuntie,' Albert'd said.

Frank'd let me go and he'd turned to face Albert.

'Come on then,' Albert'd said. 'Put 'em up.'

For a minute I'd thought Frank was going to stick up for himself. But he hadn't tried to do anything. Albert had given him three or four quick punches that had put him on the floor and made his nose bleed. Frank had sat up and taken out his handkerchief and wiped his nose. I remember that seeing him do that made me realise something I'd always been aware of but never thought about; Frank always carried a clean handkerchief.

Then Albert had turned and walked away and his gang had followed. When he'd got as far as the door he'd paused. 'Come on Yukker,' he'd said. 'Leave the pansy to his knitting circle.'

I'd looked down at Frank. He'd made no attempt to get up. He'd been looking at the spots on his handkerchief and at Albert's words he'd looked up at me but he'd already guessed what I was going to do.

At that time, Albert Swift had been very good looking. He'd had black hair, well greased, and long sideboards. His teeth were white and he'd had very clear light grey eyes. The shape of his face had been sharp and square. The man who sat in the chair across the room on the other side of the kitchen table looked nothing like the man I'd known at that time. There was no hair on the top of his head though he still had his sideboards. His teeth were very brown. The

130

sharp, clean features had sunk without trace, hidden behind lined fish-coloured skin. His eyes had a yellow tint and glowed red at the edges.

After he'd spoken, he sat there for a bit staring at me and the room while it sank in that Jack Carter was actually there standing in the room, living and breathing. Then when it finally got through he started to get up. No, that's not quite right – an exaggeration. He gave the impression he was going to get up but there was no movement significant enough for you to be able to guess that that was what he was going to do. His shirt might have creased a little bit but that was about all.

I walked round the kitchen table.

'Don't get up, Albert,' I said.

Mentally he sank back in his chair. I opened out a metal garden chair that was propped up against the table and sat down and lit a fag.

Albert didn't look very well at all.

'How are you keeping, Albert,' I said.

'Not too bad,' he said. 'You know.'

There was a silence.

'Jack Carter,' he said. 'Who'd have thought it?'

'Didn't you know I was in town?'

'Well, you know, I don't get out any more, Jack.' He tapped his chest. 'Me tubes. I stop at home and keep warm. I only get to know

131

what Lucille tells me.'

I looked at the woman in curlers who was still staring at the television.

'No,' he said, 'Lucille, the wife – that's Greer, her sister.'

Greer carried on with her staring.

'I didn't know you'd got married, Albert,' I said.

'Well…' he said. 'I mean, you have to, don't you?' he smiled in a certain way. 'You get too old for work, don't you.'

'What are you doing these days then?' I asked.

'Nowt much. This and that. Anything I can fix up without getting out of me chair.'

'You're very lucky,' I said.

'Not really,' he said. 'Not my own choosing. Doctor's orders. I miss the old life.'

There was a silence.

'You're looking good, Jack,' he said. 'Very good. I hear you're doing very well.'

'Oh, you've heard that much,' I said.

'Heard that years ago, Jack. When I was out and about.'

A door opened. The door was at the opposite end of the kitchen from where the telly was. I looked round and Albert half turned his head. A man and a woman came through the door. The man was wearing a donkey jacket and overalls. He had a knapsack over his shoulder. He lit a fag as he came through the door. The woman was wearing a man's tartan dressing gown. I wouldn't know what she was wearing underneath. Her hair was ginger and naturally it was in curlers. She was already half-way down a Woodbine. The man in the donkey jacket began to walk towards the back door. The old bird who'd let me in had been sitting on another of those garden chairs pushed up against the kitchen table. The minute the bloke started for the door the old bird got up off her seat and stood in his way.

'Would you like to give something to Ma?' said the woman in the man's dressing gown.

The bloke stopped and put his fag in his mouth and undid his donkey jacket, took a roll of notes out of the top pocket of his overalls, peeled off a ten bob note and gave it to the old bird. The old bird took the money and sat down again without saying anything. The bloke continued on his way to the door.

'Goodnight, Len,' said Albert. 'See you again.'

The bloke nodded and went to open the door but before he could get his hand to it the oldest of the little girls jumped up from the floor and shot across the kitchen and opened it for him.

'Goodnight, goodnight, goodnight,' she shrieked, grinning all over her face.

133

'Goodnight,' the bloke said to her, and went out. The little girl beamed all round the room and went and sat down again.

'Jack,' said Albert, 'meet the wife. Lucille, this is Jack Carter. Friend of mine from the old days.'

''Lo,' said Lucille.

'Pleased to meet you,' I said. I didn't stand up.

She walked round the table and got a chair that had been standing underneath the window and put it next to the stool where Greer was sitting.

''Lo, Lucille,' said Greer.

''Lo, Greer,' said Lucille.

'I've brought Club,' said Greer and reached down to her shopping bag that was on the floor by her stool and took out one of those big mail order catalogues and she and Lucille began to go through it. Albert threw his fag into the fireplace and took his packet out of his cardigan pocket and offered one to me but I was already on. He took one for himself and lit up. Outside there was the sound of a motor cycle starting up.

'You heard about Frank, of course,' I said.

'Yes,' he said, inhaling. 'Bad business.'

'You think so?' I said.

'Why yes,' he said.

'What do you know about it, Albert?' I said.

'What do I know about it?'

134

'That's right.'

'What I saw in the paper. That's what I know about it. Same as everybody else.'

'Stop playing silly buggers, Albert. You know Frank was finished off on purpose.'

Albert looked me straight in the eyes.

'That's a very interesting remark, Jack,' he said.

'Put it another way; if Frank was knocked off then you'd know that that was the case. Wouldn't you? Just as you knew I was in town and just as you'd know that I wouldn't leave until I'd squared things up. And I know Frank was knocked off. So there you are.'

Albert blew out a lot of smoke.

'It doesn't really matter if you don't want to tell me anything, Albert,' I said, 'because I'd understand. But do me a favour. Don't play silly buggers.'

Albert looked towards Lucille and Greer but our talk was strained by the row from the telly and their own chatter so there was no need for him to worry.

'Jack,' he said, 'all I know is that it struck me as being a bit funny. Knowing Frank. The circumstances, like. But if I did know anything for certain that summat like that'd happened, then you know it would be very hard for me to tell you anything about it.'

There was a silence.

'Who was it, Albert?' I said after a while.

135

Albert kept looking at me. He didn't say anything.

'All right,' I said. 'I shan't ask you again.'

I lit up a fresh fag.

'Then tell us this; who's Thorpey working for these days?'

Albert inhaled.

'Thorpey?' he said. 'Steelworks Thorpey?'

'Steelworks Thorpey.'

'Isn't he still working for himself, then?'

'I wouldn't know, would I?'

Albert went into the business of looking as if he was trying to remember when he'd last heard owt about Thorpey.

'No,' he said eventually, 'the last I heard he was still working for himself. I think that must have been, oh, six months ago.'

I looked at him.

'Straight up, Jack,' he said. 'As far as I know Thorpey still works for himself.'

'Then why the fucking hell would he be wanting to know where to find me?'

'Maybe he's got something to tell you.'

'My mother's fat arse. Remember that fracas at Skeggie?'

Albert didn't say anything for a minute.

'Well in that case, maybe he wants to get to you before you get to him.'

'Why should a little squit like Thorpey knock off Frank? Besides, he wouldn't have the guts. He'd pee his pants if you so much as looked at him.'

Albert shrugged.

'Well, I don't know, Jack,' he said.

'Yes you do, Albert,' I said. 'But I don't expect you to tell me, even if it's only an idea. But Thorpey's different. Just who's he working for?'

'Jack, I've told you. As far as I know he's still working for himself.'

'As far as you know,' I said.

I stood up and threw my cigarette in the hearth.

'Well,' I said, 'thanks, Albert. You've been a big help. You must let me know if I can do you a favour sometime.'

Albert put on a weary face.

'Think what you like, Jack,' he said. 'I can't say I know something if I don't.'

'That's right, Albert,' I said.

I walked over to the door.

'Well, don't forget,' said Albert, 'any time you're up again, drop in. We can talk over the old days.'

'I'll do that,' I said.

'Goodnight, goodnight, goodnight,' shouted the little girl.

I closed the door behind me.

The club was crowded. Old men sat riveted by dominoes. Young men thronged the six dart boards. There was no music, no singing, no women. Just the bad lighting and the good dark brown beer and the plain

137

floor and a bar that was decorated only by some barrels of beer lined up at one end.

I looked round the room. The man I'd come to see was in the same corner he'd been in the last time I'd seen him.

I went over to his table. Nobody else was sitting with him.

He would have been a thin man if it hadn't been for the size of his gut. Cider and Guinness had given him a barrage balloon for a stomach. It hung over the edge of the seat looking as though it needed a crutch to support it. A walking stick was propped between his legs. Both his hands were folded on the handle of the stick. His eyes were dead behind round gold rimmed glasses. His tongue regularly darted out of his mouth and flicked this way and that along his lips like a tiddler under water. He smelt of what he drank.

I sat down beside him

'What do you know, Rowley?' I said.

The tongue darted along his lips.

'What do you want to know?' he said.

'Who killed Frank,' I said.

'The Demon Drink,' said old Rowley. 'That's what I heard.'

He took one hand off his walking stick and adjusted his glasses.

'It'd be worth it if you knew,' I said.

'Don't know that, Jack,' said old Rowley. 'Don't know that.'

'Think of all the mucky books you could buy if you had a few quid,' I said.

'Don't know anything about Frank,' he said but his eyes weren't quite so dead as they had been.

'You know there's something to know, though. Don't you?'

'There's always something to know, Jack.'

'All right,' I said. 'Who does Thorpey work for these days?'

He didn't answer.

'A few quid,' I said. 'Keep you in books for weeks.'

He took a sip of his cider and Guinness.

'Thorpey?'

'Thorpey.'

'Rayner pays him now and then to do the odd jobs,' said old Rowley, 'or so I hear.'

'Rayner?'

He nodded. The tongue darted. I took my wallet out and took two fivers and put them on the table. He looked at them. A hand separated itself from the walking stick. The hand began to move across the table towards the money. Just like a crab. As the hand began to close over the money I whipped the notes off the table.

'Lying old bastard,' I said.

I stood up.

'No, wait a minute,' said old Rowley. 'It's true. Ask anybody.'

'Course it's true,' I said. 'Why would you

say it if it wasn't?'

I looked at him while he watched me put the money back in my wallet.

'Ta-ra, Rowley,' I said.

He shrugged and adjusted his glasses again. I left him to his smell.

I drove back into town. I was feeling dry. The scotch was back at the digs. I thought I'd drop in and have a drink and a think and then take it from there. The night was young. The pubs were only just chucking out. The Chinese restaurants would be filling up, just like the wash bowls in the Gents at the Baths where there was a dance and a bar till one o'clock every Friday night. Waltzing till ten, fighting till one. Spot fights. Progressive Barn Punch-Ups. Quicksteps in and out of the groin.

I drove past the Baths which were on the corner of the High Street and the street where my digs were. Yobboes were marching up the steps of the Baths in groups of half-a-dozen at a time. Hands in pockets, jackets open. Open-necked shirts and Walker Brothers' hair cuts.

I turned left and slowed down and backed the car into the drive and got out. All the windows at the Baths were open to let the sweat out and the sound of the group was an ebbing muffled blast in the cold night air. Dave Dee, Dozy, Beaky, Mick and Tich were as precise as a Mozart quartet against these boys.

I locked the car and began to walk back to the pavement on my way round to the front door. There was a sound of footsteps. Running. I stood at the edge of the drive, out of sight of the approaching runner. The steps were closer. A figure shot past the end of the driveway. It was Keith. I grabbed his arm and pulled him off the pavement.

'Fuck me,' he said between gasps. 'You frightened the fucking life out of me.'

He was sweating like a pig. There was the start of a bruise above his right eye. The knot in his tie was somewhere up behind his left ear. The sleeve of his jacket and the knees of his trousers had damp and gravel on them. He didn't have a lot of skin left on the knuckles on his right hand.

'What's up?' I said.

There was the sound of a car screaming round the end of the street. Abruptly the sound was reduced as the car slowed right down. The soft noise got closer.

'Thorpey,' said Keith. 'They were waiting in car park. They thought it'd be easy.'

'Was there many?'

'Four of them.'

'Including Thorpey?'

He nodded.

'Three then,' I said.

An old Zodiac slid past the driveway at

about two miles an hour, two wheels up the pavement. Four faces gaped into the darkness where we stood. The car stopped. It blocked the exit to the driveway. Nobody got out.

'Hang about,' I said to Keith.

The nearside back window was wound down.

'Jack?' said Thorpey's voice.

'Good evening,' I said.

'Like a word with you, Jack,' he said. He didn't sound very happy.

'That's nice,' I said.

'Confidential, like.'

'Stay in the car and I'll come and listen.'

'All right.'

I walked the short distance to the car and bathed myself in yellow light. I leant forward and rested my arm on the open window.

'What do you want to tell me, Thorpey?' I said.

Thorpey shoved his shaky claw out of the window. There was something in it.

'I've been asked to give you this,' he said.

He dropped the something into my hand. It was a British Railways ticket to London. I smiled.

'Train goes at four minutes past twelve,' he said. 'You've just got time.'

'Well that's very kind of somebody,' I said. 'Who do I have to thank?'

Thorpey said nothing. His ratty eyes glittered yellow in the dark of the car.

'What happens if I miss the train?' I said.

'I've been asked to make sure you don't,' he said.

His voice was getting braver by the minute but not quite brave enough.

'Oh?' I said. 'Getting optimistic in your old age, aren't you, Thorpey?'

'Let's stop fucking about,' said a voice nearest me in the front.

'Are you coming, Jack?' said Thorpey. 'It'd be best.'

I let the ticket fall to the ground.

'Right lads,' said Thorpey.

Three doors opened. Thorpey's wasn't one of them. The bloke who'd wanted to get on with it started to climb out of the front seat. I grabbed the door handle and pulled the door wide open and with all my force slammed the door into him before he could do anything about it. I timed it just right. He was half-way in and half-way out. The top edge of the door caught him on his forehead and on part of the bridge of his nose and the side edge caught a knee cap. He was very hard hit. He fell back across the front seats and started being sick. I jumped on to the bonnet of the car and kicked the driver on the side of his head before he'd had time to turn round completely after getting out of his seat. He went over but

143

only for a minute. The third bloke was squaring himself up. I jumped down off the bonnet into the street. He made the mistake of coming to me instead of letting me go to him. He swung at me and I took hold of his arm one handed and pulled him to me giving him a fore-arm smash in the wind-pipe with my other arm. He went down trying to catch hold of the breath he'd just lost. I gave him one for luck on the back of his neck. His face hit the concrete before any of the rest of him. I turned back to see the bloke I'd kicked. He'd got up but Keith was there giving him a boxer's right but while my back was turned Thorpey had wriggled out of the car and was off down the road like a frightened rabbit.

'Thorpey!' I roared.

He kept going.

I got into the car. There was no time to turn round or to shove out the bloke lying across the seat so I sat down on him. I pressed the starter and put the car into reverse. I caught up with Thorpey at the end of the street but he turned right into the High Street. I couldn't reverse round the corner so I got out and ran after him. There were plenty of people about but neither me nor Thorpey was particularly interested in them in the way that they were interested in us.

The mistake Thorpey made was to decide

to go and hide in the Baths. Fucking hell I thought at first when I saw him racing up the steps but the next minute his foot slipped and he was flat on his bloody face sliding down them again. A few people burst out laughing when they saw it happen but they soon stopped when they saw me rush up and turn him over and pull him up on to his feet. It wasn't so much that as stopped them but the short jab I gave to Thorpey's ribs.

'Now then,' I said. 'What was that confidential information you were going to tell me about?'

'Don't Jack,' he said. 'Don't Jack. It wasn't my idea, honest.'

'Right,' I said. 'Let's go and find out who's bloody idea it was then.'

I told hold of his collar and tie and started to pull him after me down the steps. Somebody pushed me hard in the chest.

'What do you think you're playing at?' a voice said.

A yobboe was standing in front of me, a step below me, and below him was another yobboe. They were both looking up into my face with much interest.

'Nothing you'd be interested in,' I said.

'Oh, yes?' he said. Then to Thorpey: 'What's up, Mate? Do you want any help?'

Thorpey didn't know what the bloody hell to say.

'Look, fellers,' I said. 'Don't get yourself into something you can't get yourself out of.'

'Oh, yes?' said the yobboe.

I started to walk down the steps again. The yobboe pushed me in the chest again. Only harder this time.

'He's littler than you are,' the yobboe said.

'So are you,' I said, 'so why chance it?'

The yobboe drew back to have a go. He thought the movement made him look tough but all it did was make him slow. I gave him one in the stomach. His Walker Brother's hairstyle flopped over his face and he sank to his knees on the steps. His mate watched him go all the way down then slowly turned his gaze on me.

'Do you want some?' I said. 'Or do you only work as a double act?'

The yobboe didn't answer. I walked past him and his mate who by now was resting his forehead on one of the steps trying to remember how he happened to get such a terrible pain in his gut. Nobody else stood in my way and so I walked on leaving the lights from the inside of the Baths streaming over the praying yobboe on the steps. Thorpey, of course, walked with me. I let go of him only when we turned into the street where my digs were.

The car was where I'd left it. One of Thorpey's boys was helping the boyo I'd given the forearm to into the back seat. The one giving the helping hand looked at me and Thorpey but that was all. Then he went round the other side of the car and lifted the legs of the boyo on the front seat and packed them away under the dashboard. After he'd done that, he got into the driving seat and did what I didn't do; he reversed very quickly into the High Street. Thorpey was very sensible. He didn't run screaming after the car. Keith was standing on the pavement outside my digs talking to a woman. The woman was my landlady. Across the street there were lights on that hadn't been on before.

'Now then,' said my landlady when I got there, 'just what the bloody hell do you think you're on?'

'I'm very sorry,' I said.

'You look it,' she said.

'No, I am, really,' I said.

'Don't come that bloody flannel with me,' she said. 'If you're a travelling man, I'm bloody Twiggy. What the 'ell's going on. And who's he?'

Thorpey continued to be at a loss for words. An elderly woman wrapped inside a dressing gown traipsed across the road:

'What's going on? Have you no thought for others?' she shouted. Her thin voice was whipped away by the wind and carried off above the street lights.

'Maybe if we went inside it'd be better,' I said.

'Inside?' said my landlady. 'Why should I give house-room to your sort?'

'Everybody knows you, Edna Garfoot,' shouted the old woman. 'Everybody knew there'd be trouble. This is a respectable street.'

I looked at my landlady and smiled. My landlady frowned. She turned to the old woman:

'You keep your bloody trap shut, Ma,' she said.

'Oh! Oh!' said the old woman. 'I'll send my old man over to see you.'

'Yes, and wouldn't he love it, you dried up old biddy,' said my landlady.

'Oh!' said the old woman. 'Oh!'

She began to retreat across the street. I nodded to Keith and gave Thorpey a shove. We went into the house.

'Here!' said my landlady. She rushed up the path. We waited for her in the hall. She didn't close the door.

'Well?' she said.

'Well,' I said, 'you might as well close the door. We're in now.'

She glared at me for a minute then breathed in and closed the door. Keith and Thorpey and me began to go upstairs.

'Where do you think you're going?' she said.

'To my room,' I said. 'We've got one or two things to talk over.'

She followed us up the stairs.

'What are you going to do?' she said.

I opened the door to my room.

'Why don't you go and make us all a nice cup of tea?' I said.

I nodded to Keith. Keith bundled Thorpey into the room.

'What are you going to do?' she said again.

I closed the door in her face and locked it.

'Make us a nice cup of tea and I'll tell you,' I said. 'I might even let you come in and watch.'

'I'll call the police,' she said.

'No you won't,' I said.

There was a silence.

'Don't worry,' I said. 'Nothing's going to happen. Just get us that tea.'

There was more silence, eventually the silence of her going away.

Keith and Thorpey were standing in the middle of the room. Keith had his hands in his trouser pockets. He was looking at me. Thorpey was looking at me too but he didn't have his hands in his pockets. He was standing to attention looking like somebody from the British Legion. His thumbs were turned down following the lines where the uniform stripes would have been.

'Sit down, Thorpey,' I said.

He didn't move.

'Relax,' I said. 'Keith, get Thorpey a chair.'

Keith got the chair that my landlady had displayed herself on earlier in the day. He put the chair down in the middle of the room behind Thorpey.

Thorpey remained standing.

I rooted in my hold-all and got a bottle out and also my flask.

I unscrewed the cap of the flask and very carefully poured in some scotch from the bottle. I handed the flask to Keith and sat down on the bed. Keith took a pull and I took off my jacket and loosened the laces in my shoes.

Thorpey remained standing.

I took a big drink from the bottle. I put it down on the floor and took my fags out and offered one to Keith. We lit up.

'Well now, Thorpey,' I said.

He didn't say anything.

'Seems I've got a secret benefactor,' I said.

I took another drink. Thorpey watched the bottle on its way up from the floor into my mouth and down to the floor again.

'It's a very nice thing to know is that,' I said. 'Isn't it Keith?'

Keith didn't answer. He didn't nod either. I got the feeling he was worried about something.

'Trouble is about a secret benefactor,' I said, 'not knowing who he is, it makes you feel a bit embarrassed, like. I mean, there's no way you can say Ta, is there?'

Thorpey was still gazing at the bottle.

'There's also this about it,' I said. 'A benefactor like that, well, you get to wondering why they've picked on you. I mean, out of all the needy cases there are about these days.'

There was silence.

'I'd like to know who it is, Thorpey.'

Nothing.

'All right, all right,' I said wearily. 'If you like, we'll stop mucking about. Somebody sent you to put me on a train because they're shit scared of me sticking my nose in something or other and I've a good idea of the something or other they don't want my nose in. If I'm right then one or two people are going to be in quite a little bit of trouble. Now, I don't know, but you might be one of them. If you are, God help you. Because if you are, I'll find out. But you may not know anything about it at all. Maybe all you know is that somebody gave you a bundle of fivers to do a job. What I want you to tell me more than anything else is who gave you the bundle of fivers.'

Thorpey looked at me.

'I can't Jack,' he said. 'How can I?'

'Yes you can, Thorpey.'

'Honest, mate, I can't.'

'Come on now. You know it's for the best.'

He looked at the floor and shook his head.

'Did you have anything to do with it, Thorpey?' I said.

'What?'

'Frank.'

'What?'

'Were you there?'

'When?'

'When they poured the whisky down his throat?'

'What?'

'Did you hold the bottle?'

'What?'

There was a knock on the door. I nodded to Keith. He let her in. She was carrying a tea tray.

'Did you have a good laugh when he was sicking it up as fast as you could pour it down him?'

Thorpey stared at me.

'Was it a giggle when you let out the hand brake and Frank's car started rolling down top road?'

His head began to shake.

'Did you all pass the bottle round after the car went through the hedge? The same bottle you'd shoved halfway down his throat?'

'I don't know what you're talking about, Jack,' said Thorpey.

'Well, I do,' I said.

I jumped off the bed and grabbed Thorpey's scruffy neck and shoved him back on to the chair.

'I'm talking about me bloody brother, Thorpey. That's what I'm talking about. So bloody well start spouting or else!'

Thorpey kept staring up into my face so I let him have three across it. He raised his arms to cover his head and said:

'No, don't, Jack. Don't.'

'Who killed him, Thorpey?'

'I don't know. I don't know.'

'But you know he was killed.'

'No. No.'

'Who asked you to get me out of it?'

He shook his head. I hit him again, a low uppercut connecting smack in the middle of his bowed head.

'No, don't hit us, Jack,' he said.

'Then tell us.'

'All right. All right,' he said. 'I'll tell you.'

I stood back. He stayed perched on the edge of the seat, still crouching forward.

'Brumby,' he said. 'He gave us the money. But that's all I know. Honest.'

'What did he say to you?'

'He just said find out where you were and make sure you caught twelve o'clock train.'

'Is that all?'

'That's all. Honest, Jack.'

'Did the boyos know where the money was coming from?'

'No, only me.'

I went back to the bed and sat down.

'Brumby eh?' I said.

'But for Christ's sake don't tell him I said so, Jack. Please.'

'Do you work for him all the time these days?' I said.

'No,' he said. 'Just the odd jobs.'

'He wouldn't have paid you to do something for him recently would he? Like say last Sunday?'

'Honest, Jack, that's all. Honest.'

I took a drink. My landlady was still standing in front of the door holding the tea tray.

'Ah, that's nice,' I said. 'Just what we all need. A nice cup of tea.'

She didn't look quite so indignant as she'd looked before. She put the tray down on the dressing table and began to pour the tea out.

'Brumby,' I said again.

'Can I go now?' said Thorpey.

'No, you bloody well can't,' I said.

'Who's Brumby?' said Keith.

'Cliff Brumby?' I said. 'Ever been to Cleethorpes?'

Keith nodded.

'Ever walked into an arcade and put a penny in a slot machine?'

'Yes,' said Keith.

'Well, ten to one the slot machine belongs to Brumby and like as not the bloody arcade as well. Same in Brid and Skeggie. Isn't that right, Thorpey?'

154

Thorpey didn't answer.

'Where does Cliff hang out these days, Thorpey?'

No reply.

'Thorpey?'

'You might find him at the Conservative Club. He goes there most Fridays. He's a snooker player.'

'And where does he live?'

'He's got a house at Burnham.'

'What's the address?'

No reply.

'Thorpey?'

'House is called "Pantiles". He had it built a year or so ago.'

'Well,' I said. 'Thanks very much.'

My landlady gave me a cup of tea.

'Thanks very much Mrs Garfoot. Or may I call you Edna?'

'Suppose you tell me just what the bloody hell's going on. It is my house you know.'

I poured some whisky into my tea and stirred it up.

'Yes,' I said. 'You've been very good about the whole thing, Edna, you really have.'

'Stick the soft soap. Let's be having it.'

I drank my tea and stood up.

'Can't explain right now,' I said. 'Have to go out for a bit. Keith'll put you in the picture.'

'Keith?'

'Oh,' I said shrugging on my jacket. 'I'm

155

ever so sorry. Edna, Keith. Keith, Edna.'

'Who says he's staying here?' said my landlady.

'Well, he has to, doesn't he? Till I come back. Make sure Thorpey doesn't walk out and make a couple of phone calls.'

'Oh, heck,' said Thorpey.

'Now just a minute...' said my landlady.

'Ta-ra,' I said. 'Oh and Keith, ta very much. You've been a big help. I'll see you're all right. O.K. mate?'

Keith half smiled.

'Right mate,' he said.

I closed the door and went down the stairs.

I tried the Conservative Club first.

There was no receptionist this time. I walked straight in. There was a badly lit hallway with two fruit machines standing on either side like sentries. Nobody was playing them. Rooms with closed doors lined the hallway. At the far end were some double doors and beyond those doors there were the sounds of snooker. I walked down the hall and through the doors.

There were six tables, all occupied. The ceiling was very very high and the table lights looked a bit daft suspended on their thin wires that went upwards through the acres of darkness. There was a raised platform about a foot high going round the whole of the room and on this platform there were benches flush to the wall so that the non-players could sit and watch the players. Brumby was among neither of these two groups. Apart from the lights above the tables the only bright light in the room was in one corner and it came from the tiny curved bar at which the steward leaned, his chin cupped in his hands, watching the game on the table nearest the bar. That is, until he saw me.

Then he straightened up and frowned. He was about to lift the bar flap and come through to say a few words to me but I didn't give him the chance. I was at the bar before you could say 'Members Only'.

'I'm very sorry to intrude like this,' I said, 'but I have an urgent message for a Mr Brumby. Could you tell me where I'm likely to find him?'

'This is very irregular,' he said. 'We never allow non-members unaccompanied into the club.'

'No, I know,' I said. 'Like I said, I'm sorry to intrude like this, but it is rather urgent.'

'And nobody's allowed in after eleven,' he said.

'No,' I said. 'I know. But you see I was told Mr Brumby might be here and it's a matter that really could do with his attention...'

'To do with his business is it?' said the nosey old bugger.

'No, not exactly,' I said. 'But it is rather urgent.'

'Who are you?' he said.

'A friend of Mr Brumby's. Now...'

'Never seen you before.'

'No. I've just driven up from London.'

'Oh, yes?'

I began to walk away from the bar.

'Where do you think you're going?' he said.

'To look for Mr Brumby.'

'Well, it's no good looking here,' he said. 'Mr Brumby hasn't been in tonight.'

I turned round.

'Oh?' I said.

'No,' he said. 'Not tonight. It's the Police Ball, isn't it?'

The night was very black and the roads were very narrow. The windscreen wipers droned on and on. I looked at my watch. The luminous hands said ten past one. If the dance finished at one o'clock it would take him about thirty-five to forty minutes to drive out to Burnham. I'd be ahead of him by about twenty minutes. If the dance didn't finish until half-past one or two o'clock then I'd have a long wait. But I didn't mind that.

The road dipped and the headlights picked out the sign that said Burnham. I slowed down. It was only a small village and I didn't want to miss the house.

There wasn't much chance of that. I stopped the car and wound the window down. Set back from the road on quite a steep rise was a new ranch-style house. All the lights were on. There were a lot of cars parked in the drive and up and down the road. A lot of noise was going on inside but I couldn't hear much of it. I could only see the people who were making it. The house was packed with kids. A little party for the offspring while Mummy and Daddy kissed the Chief Inspector's bum. Well, there wasn't much point in ringing that musical doorbell for a while. I backed the car up on to the grass verge on the opposite side of the road to the house and lit a fag and watched and waited. A few people came out and got into cars and went and one young bloke came out on all fours and was sick all over the Begonias but apart from that nothing much happened except that the insides of the windows got steamier and the music got noisier.

About quarter to two a nice new Rover crept down the road and turned into the drive. The car braked abruptly in the middle of the gateway. The engine was turned off. Nothing happened for a minute or two. Then the passenger door opened and Cliff Brumby got out. He looked very nice. He had on a beautiful dark double-breasted overcoat which he wore undone and draped round his shoulders was a tasselled white silk scarf. His height added to his elegant appearance as did his beautifully barbered greying hair. He looked more like Henry Cabot Lodge just come from the White House than a fiddling slot machine king just come from the Police Ball.

He stood looking at the house for a full minute, not moving, his hand on the car door.

'Fuck me,' he said.

He still didn't move.

'Now Cliff,' came a woman's voice from inside the car, 'don't get mad. You'll only regret it.'

Cliff slammed the door of the car, as hard as I'd slammed the door of the car on his boyo earlier in the evening.

'I'll murder the little bitch,' he said.

'Cliff...' said the woman's voice.

Cliff strolled up the drive deliberately not hurrying. He stopped once to look at the young blood sleeping among the Begonias. He looked at him for quite some time before turning away. When he got to the front door he didn't open it and simply go in. Instead, he rang the bell and stepped back and folded his arms. The musical chimes were just strident enough to separate themselves from the rest of the noise. A red dress rippled behind the full length frosted glass panel. The door opened. The girl was very pretty. Her eyes were very bright and her cheeks were very red and she looked very happy until she saw who was standing there before her.

'Daddy,' she said.

'That's right,' he said. 'Bloody Daddy.'

'But it's only quarter to two,' she said thinking out loud. 'The dance doesn't finish till two o'clock.'

'That's right,' he said. 'Perhaps this'll teach you never to bet on certainties.'

The girl's face began to crumble.

'And this is what you call having a few friends in for coffee is it?' said Cliff.

'Oh-h,' the girl said.

Cliff began to walk past her into the house.

'Running bloody riot over my bloody furniture, drinking my bloody booze, spewing all over my...'

The rest was lost as he disappeared inside. The door on the driver's side of the Rover opened and the woman got out. She was wearing a white evening dress, very plain and beautiful, and a mink coat, also very plain and beautiful. The trouble was, she was fat, so the beautiful dress and the beautiful coat didn't really matter very much. She stood there watching the house and chewing herself up. I couldn't see a bloke like Cliff spending more hours a day with her than he had to.

People started pouring out of the house. The music stopped. Cars started. Cliff was visible through the windows as he went from room to room directing operations. Finally he appeared at the door, helping out a boy and a girl holding them by the scruffs of their necks. The girl looked very rumpled and the boy was having trouble with his fly which had somehow got jammed.

After Cliff had propelled this particular couple on their way, he wandered over to the Begonias and picked up the young blood and carried him down the drive and dropped him on the grass verge by the gateway.

'Cliff, be careful,' said the woman.

'Shut up,' said Cliff.

He walked back to the house. The woman followed. Cliff stood to one side to let the last few people leave. He looked into the face of each one of them as they passed him. When they'd gone he went into the house.

'Sandra!'

It was a wonder his double glazing stayed intact. The woman went into the house and closed the door but I could still hear Cliff's voice.

'Sandra!'

There was a silence then I saw Cliff appear beyond one of the upstairs windows. He stood with his back to the window looking down at a point out of sight inside the bedroom. He began shouting again.

I got out of the car and closed the door.

I crossed the road and walked up the drive. I stood outside the front door for a few moments. Cliff was still delivering his spiel upstairs. The rest of the house was silent. There was no sound of glasses being moved or ashtrays being emptied or furniture being straightened.

I opened the front door and closed it behind me without making any noise at all.

I was in a square hall. It wasn't big and it wasn't small. A fitted carpet washed across the floor and its floral pattern was far too big to fit into the space it occupied. There was a low staircase, central to the hall, that turned at right angles three times before it reached the balcony that ran all the way around the four walls. The banisters and balcony railings were white-glossed wrought iron. The wallpaper was floral, too. The pattern was not much smaller than the pattern on the carpet. There was a print of the green-faced Oriental Girl in a white frame on one of the walls and on another wall high up there was a pair of plastic duelling pistols. In one corner near the front door was a glass topped wrought iron telephone table with a red telephone on it. All the doors leading off the hall had full length panels of frosted glass set into them. One of the doors was open. Without moving from the front door I looked through it. I could see the whole of a big white armchair and part of a matching sofa. Beyond the sofa, I could see part of a farmhouse-style brick-fronted fireplace with an electric fire set in the middle of it. The fire was just warming up. On the mantelpiece there were lots of glasses and ashtrays. Above the glasses and ashtrays there was Flatford Mill.

I walked into the room. Mrs Brumby was sitting at the end of the sofa that had previously been out of sight. She still had her coat on. She was looking at the bars of the electric fire. Her elbow was resting on the arm of the sofa and her fingers were slowly stroking her forehead, as if she was trying to get rid of a mild headache. She didn't notice me at first.

'Good evening,' I said.

At first all she did was to turn her head slowly as if she wasn't aware of anything out of the ordinary, but when she saw me she stood up very quickly and knocked an ashtray off the arm of the sofa.

'I'm sorry I startled you,' I said. 'I pressed the bell but nothing happened. So as the door was open...'

'Who are you?' she said.

'I'm sorry,' I said. 'The name's Carter. Jack Carter.'

'Have you come about the noise?'

'No, no,' I said. 'I'm an old friend of

Cliff's. I thought I'd drop in as there's something I'd like to talk to him about.'

At first there was slight relief in her face then her subsequent expressions described what was going through her mind. An old friend. From the old days. At this time of night. She looked at her watch, then up to the ceiling. Cliff's voice droned on and on.

'I know it's a bit of an odd time to be calling,' I said. 'But it is rather urgent.'

'What do you want to see Cliff about?'

'Well, actually, it is business…' I said.

'I know all about Cliff's business,' she said.

'I'm sure,' I said.

'Well?'

'Look, Mrs Brumby,' I said. 'I'm not acting for myself, understand. Just tell Cliff Jack Carter from London's here to see him.'

She raised her chin a bit and looked at me.

'How am I supposed to know it's business?' she said. 'Why should I take your word for it. I don't know.'

'But you know Gerald and Les Fletcher, don't you?' I said.

She looked at me some more and I could tell she believed I was with Gerald and Les. But she didn't know what to believe about why I was there. But whatever the reason she knew I wouldn't be leaving until I'd seen Cliff. So she concentrated her look for a bit longer and then walked quickly out of the room and up the stairs.

I looked round the room. Over on the other side of the room in front of the picture window that looked out on to I don't know what was a reproduction refectory table with matching dining chairs. The table was awash with drink. Empty Pipkins took up a third of the table top. The rest was just glasses and booze from Cliff's musical cocktail cabinet. On one edge of the table a cigarette had burned a nice little groove in the polished oak.

Upstairs things were happening. The voices were now droning on, but much softer. Then there was quiet. A door opened and closed. Footsteps ruffled the stair carpet. Cliff Brumby came into the room. I turned to face him. He didn't look very pleased at all. I don't think I could have been looking too happy either because there was something stirring down in my gut, a feeling I didn't like very much. It had something to do with my looking at Cliff's face and seeing what I saw there.

'What the fucking hell's all this?' he said.

I didn't say anything.

'I suppose you know what the bloody time is?'

I nodded. He told me anyway.

'It's quarter past two in the bloody morning.'

'I know.'

'Well?'

I took out my fags and lit one.

'Dot told me the Fletchers sent you. What's so bloody important it can't wait till the morning?'

I shook my head.

'No,' I said. 'The Fletchers didn't send me.'

He looked at me. Then he walked forward and clenched his fist and pointed his index finger at my face about an inch from my nose.

'Now look,' he said. 'Just bloody look. I'm not in the mood tonight. I've had it. Right up to here. So let's not try and be too funny, eh? Because I don't feel much like bloody laughing.'

'I made a mistake,' I said.

'What?'

'I said it looks as if I've made a mistake.'

'A mistake? About what?'

'I was given some wrong information.'

'Wrong information? What about?'

'I was given some wrong information about you. I've known it was wrong since you came into this room.'

Cliff sat down on the arm of the sofa. Things were dawning.

'It wasn't business, was it?'

'No, it wasn't business,' I said.

There was a silence. Things dawned on him.

167

'You came here to do me. Is that it?'

I didn't say anything.

'What for, Jack?'

'I'd rather not say.'

'You'd rather not say?'

'Cliff, I made a mistake. I've got to get back. See somebody about something.'

I began to walk over to the door. Cliff whisked up from the sofa and grabbed my lapels.

'Now just you bloody well look here. I don't like hard cases walking in and out of my house in the middle of the night threatening to do me. You're not leaving here until you've explained your bloody self. You came here to do me and I want to know what for. If somebody's been putting something about about me, I want to know who the fucking hell it is. And when I know what it is and who's been saying it, I just might want to take the mater up with you, Jack, mightn't I?'

'You might,' I said. 'And then again, you might not.'

'Meaning?'

'Cliff, you're a big bloke – you're in good shape. But I know more than you do.'

It wasn't exactly the best thing I could have said. Cliff swung me round with all his strength and flung me down on the settee. He leant over me and only just managed to stop himself from smashing my face in.

'Now then, cuntie,' he said. 'Let's be having you.'

I let him have me. I kicked him hard on his shin and gave him one in his gut, not too hard, but hard enough. I stood up. This time it was my turn with the lapels. I straightened him up and looked into his face. It was slightly greyer than it had been before.

'Sorry about that,' I said. 'Some things go against the grain.'

I walked out of the room. Mrs Brumby was standing stock still on the stairs.

'Goodnight,' I said.

I opened the front door. Mrs Brumby ran into the front room.

'What happened?' I heard her say. 'Are you all right? Who was it? What did he want?'

'None of your bloody business.'

'There was trouble wasn't there?'

'Isn't it about time you started clearing up the bloody mess your daughter's made?'

A slight pause.

'Yes, Cliff. I suppose it is.'

I closed the door as quietly as I'd done when I'd come in.

I backed the car into the garage and walked round to the front door of the boarding house. It was open. Only a few inches, but it was open.

I didn't make any noise. The light was still

169

on, illuminating the air a few feet round the bulb and nothing else. There was no sound in the house.

I walked over to the foot of the stairs. The door into the kitchen at the end of the hall opened slightly. Whoever was in the kitchen preferred to be in there without any lights on.

I turned from the foot of the stairs and walked quickly down the hall and pushed the kitchen door wide open. It opened in-wards. The door bumped against whoever it was who'd begun to open it. I felt inside the doorway and flicked the light switch. There was a small scream. I yanked the door back and slammed it to behind me. My landlady was standing there trying to press herself into the wallpaper. There was a bruise under her right eye. It was going to be quite a rainbow. She was wearing a long red dress-ing gown with a wafting white feather collar. She was holding a glass and a cigarette in her left hand and in her right hand she was holding an ornamental brass poker. She looked at me and I looked at her.

'Well,' I said. 'What happened?'

She stopped looking at me and went over to the kitchen table. She picked up a bottle of brandy. It was good stuff. She poured some of the good stuff into her glass.

'They came back, didn't they?'

She took a drink.

'One of them did. With two different fellers.'

'What happened?'

'What the Christ do you think happened?'

I didn't say anything.

'They came for that bloke, didn't they? They knew you wouldn't be here. They thought it was all very funny.'

'All right,' I said. 'So what happened? What did they do to Keith?'

'They took him with them. The one who was here before wasn't very pleased with him.'

'What happened to you?'

She didn't answer.

'Well?'

'Put it this way; you owe me for a new blouse.'

'You were lucky,' I said, lighting up. I looked round the kitchen. On the wall was a whitewood cabinet. I slid the glass door back and took out a cup. I went over to the table and sat down on a kitchen chair and poured myself a brandy.

'Is that it, then?' said my landlady.

I didn't say anything.

'You don't care, do you? They could have done anything.'

I didn't say anything.

'And what about that lad? Aren't you going to do anything about it?'

'Nothing I can do, is there?'

'What'll they do to him?'

'Hard to say, offhand.'

I took a drink.

She rushed over to the kitchen door and pulled it open so that it banged on the kitchen wall.

'Get out,' she screamed. 'Get out of my house.'

I took another drink. She began to cry.

'Bloody rotten sod, you are,' she said. 'Who the hell do you think you are? They hurt me tonight. They bloody hurt me.'

'That's nothing to what they did to my brother,' I said.

'And what are you going to do? Do it back to them?'

'That's right.'

'You didn't get very far tonight, did you?'

I didn't answer.

'What happened? Did you murder the wrong man?'

'No I bloody didn't so put a sock in it.'

'Oh, they were full of it when they came to get Thorpey. Thorpey really thought it was funny.'

'Shut up.'

'He was saying as how he'd been told to tell you Brumby'd sent him if they couldn't manage you. Thorpey said he'd like to have seen Brumby's face when you tackled him.'

'And why should Brumby fix me if four of them bastards couldn't?'

'You're missing the point. They were hoping you might fix Brumby. Kill him, with a bit of luck. They know you're not the kind of bloke to ask questions first. Thorpey said it'd kill two birds with one stone. Get Brumby out of the way and you fixed for doing him at the same time. Thorpey's waiting to hear what happened so he can phone somebody he knows at Cop Shop and tell him all about it.'

'Well, he'll be disappointed, won't he?'

'What happened? Was Brumby bigger than you expected.'

I said nothing.

'Bloody brave aren't you with a little bloke like Thorpey.'

'Shut up.'

'Good job Keith was there to help you out earlier. Pity though, isn't it, that you're not there when he needs a hand.'

'Do you want something?'

'Oh, yes. You'd like that wouldn't you?'

'No, but you might.'

She rushed over to me.

'Would you like to see the bruises?'

'Why? Do you want to show me?'

She hit me across the face. I hit her back. She hit me again. I stood up and took hold of her by the wrists and swung her against the wall. I let go of her before she connected and walked out of the kitchen and down the hall and began to go up the stairs. She ran

173

out of the kitchen.

'Where do you think you're going?' she screamed.

'To bed. Coming?' I said, not stopping.

She ran to the bottom of the stairs.

'You'll get out! You'll bloody well get out! If you don't I'll call the police.'

'Sure you will,' I said going into the bedroom.

I went over to the bed and lifted the counterpane. I took the long parcel from underneath the bed and began to unwrap the newspapers. My landlady appeared in the doorway but I didn't take any notice of her. She took a lot of notice of me when she saw I was unwrapping a shotgun. I broke the gun and took the box of cartridges from the hold-all and put two up the spout.

'What are you going to do with that?' she said.

'Protect my goods and chattels.'

'They won't be back tonight? Will they?'

I snapped the gun together again.

'You never know,' I said.

'And you'd use that if they did?'

'Don't be bloody silly. You only have to point one of these to get results.'

'Then why have you loaded it?'

'Somebody might think I was bluffing. I'd like to be certain I wasn't.'

'Jesus,' she said wearily.

I leant the gun against the wall next to the

bed and stretched out and closed my eyes. I heard my landlady walk over to the bedside table and pick up one of the cups and pour something into it.

'Why did they kill your brother?' she said.

'I don't know,' I said. 'And I don't know who "they" are either.'

'Didn't Thorpey have anything to do with it then?'

'I very much doubt it. He wouldn't have the nerve.'

'He had the nerve to send you on a wild goose chase tonight.'

'That wasn't nerve; that was betting on a dead cert. I wasn't supposed to finish up back here whichever way the land lay. He'll be peeing his pants when he finds out I didn't act true to type.'

'Will you go after him?'

'I would if I thought I could catch him. He's probably half-way to Doncaster or Barnsley or somewhere by now. He won't be back until I've been gone a month.'

'What about Keith. What are you going to do about him?'

'Give him some money.'

'That's a lot of use to him right now.'

'I don't know where he lives, do I? I don't know where they've taken him, do I? Do you know?'

'No.'

'There you are then.'

175

She didn't say anything for a while. I sat up and had a big drink and lay down again and closed my eyes.

'What are you going to do if you catch who did it?' she said.

'What do you think?'

Another silence.

'Why?' she said.

'He was my brother.'

She sat down on the bed.

'You'd just kill them? Just like that?'

'If they didn't kill me first.'

'Could you do it? I mean without worrying about it?'

'Anybody could if it was their own flesh and blood as was involved and they knew they weren't going to get caught.'

'And you're not going to get caught?'

'No.'

'How do you know?'

'Because I know.'

After a little while she said:

'Supposing I phoned the police and told them that there was a bloke in my boarding house with a shotgun and he'd told me he was off to shoot somebody with it?'

'You wouldn't.'

'How do you know I wouldn't?'

'Because I know you wear green underwear.'

'What's that supposed to mean?'

'Think about it.'

She thought about it.

There was a long pause in which nothing at all happened except that I opened my eyes and found that I was looking into hers. She wasn't looking at me as though she liked me but then she didn't have to. Women that wear green underwear don't. I stretched an arm out and pulled open the front of her dressing gown. The bra matched what I'd already seen. There was a bruise near her left nipple. She kept looking at me.

'What did they do?' I said.

'One of them ripped my blouse. Another punched me. They would have gone on if Thorpey hadn't started getting worried about things.'

I touched the bruise with my finger.

'He hit you there, did he?' I said.

She didn't say anything.

'That couldn't have been very pleasant,' I said. 'Or could it?'

'You're a bastard, aren't you?'

I didn't answer, I kept massaging the bruise. Then she leant backwards so that her back was arched across my chest. She undid the cord on her dressing gown and then squirmed her arms underneath her and unhooked her bra and left her arms where they were, pinned underneath her. I extended the massaging to cover a larger area. Eventually, still lying across me, she rolled over on to her side, facing away from me.

Saturday

I woke up.

I was alone. It was daylight and it was raining. The bed was warm. I only had my shirt on. It was undone and rived up round my armpits. The door opened. My landlady backed into the room. She was carrying a tray with breakfast stuff on it. I looked at my watch. It said twenty to nine. My landlady came and sat on the bed. I sat up. She put the tray across my legs. On it there was boiled eggs and things. All I was interested in was the tea pot.

'What's this in aid of?' I said.

'Would you like me to throw it at you?'

I didn't say anything. She poured the tea out. I drank a cup and poured myself a refill.

'Well,' she said, 'aren't you going to eat it?'

'I don't eat breakfast,' I said.

'You're a real little charmer, aren't you?' she said.

I picked up my cup and she moved the tray to the part of the bed I wasn't in. I could tell from her face she wanted more. I didn't want to give her any but if she insisted I thought I'd better. For the same reason I had done last night; the sweeter she

178

was, the less danger there was of her phoning the Cop Shop if she ever saw a newspaper item she might associate with me. You never could tell.

She got into bed and we got down to it. We were going strong when the bedroom door opened.

I rolled off her very quickly. The breakfast things went all over the place. I took most of the bedclothes with me. My landlady screamed and tried to snatch the bedclothes back but she couldn't quite manage it so she carried on screaming.

Now I was on my back I could see who had opened the bedroom door.

Two men were standing there looking at us. One was fairly tall with the sort of unhandsome good looks you get on blokes in the after-shave ads. He also dressed the part. He had on a white shirt with a broad hairline red and green check pattern to it, a red knitted tie, a bottle green V-neck, twill trousers and Oxford boots. Across his shoulders was draped a fur collared waterproof and on his hands were those tiny stringy driving gloves. The only items not entirely for show were the Oxford boots.

He was smiling.

The other man was not so tall and not nearly so good looking. He had on a leather trilby and a single breasted leather coat with a tie belt. Underneath the coat was a mohair e same colour as mine. Not surprising both used the same tailor. Black hair d from under the trilby and hung over his coat collar. His hands were in his coat pockets.

He was smiling.

The good looking man in the English clothes was called Peter the Dutchman. The not so good looking man was called Con McCarty. It wasn't a big step from there to Mack the Knife.

They both worked for Gerald and Les Fletcher.

'Hello, Jack,' said Con, still smiling.

'Don't let us interrupt you. You just carry on with what you were doing,' said Peter. He was still smiling too.

My landlady had stopped screaming by now because she'd managed to cover herself up. I sat up and looked at Peter and Con.

'Don't tell me,' I said. 'Let me guess.'

Con rubbed his nose with his forefinger.

'Sorry about this,' he said. 'But there you are. Orders is orders, as they say.'

'And what orders would they be, Con?'

'Gerald called us at half-past three this morning. Just after somebody had called him. Somebody told him you'd been making a nuisance of yourself.'

I said nothing.

'So Gerald asked us if we'd drive up and ask you if you wouldn't mind coming back to London with us,' said Peter.

'He said it'd be doing him a big favour if you would,' said Con.

I said nothing.

'I mean, we appreciate why you're all steamed up,' said Con, 'and so do Gerald and Les, they really do.'

'But they have to be diplomatic,' said Peter. 'They have to take the broader view.'

Both of them were still smiling.

'Gerald and Les sent you to fetch me back,' I said.

They just went on smiling.

'One way or the other,' I said.

They didn't say anything.

'And you think you're going to do it,' I said.

Nothing but smiles.

I leapt out of the bed and picked up the shotgun and pointed it at them.

'Right,' I said. 'Right. So take me back to London.'

'Now, Jack,' said Con, 'you know it'd be best if you just got dressed and came with us.'

'I mean, we don't want to get all involved, do we?' said Peter.

I advanced on them. They stepped back a little bit. They were still smiling.

'Put it away, Jack,' said Con. 'You know you won't use it.'

'The gun he means,' said Peter.

181

'Out,' I said. 'Out, out, out!'

They bundled through the door. Con laughed.

'If Audrey could see you now,' he said.

'Out,' I said.

They started down the stairs, stumbling against one another in their mirth. I followed. In the hall Peter stopped and said:

'We'll have to take you back, Jack, whether we do it now or later.'

Con opened the front door.

'Come on Jack,' he said. ' Be reasonable.'

'Out,' I said.

They went through the front door, still smiling. I followed them. The street was slick with greasy rain. Peter's red Jag was parked by the kerb across the street from the boarding house. He loved his shiny red motor. He kept it looking very nice.

Con and Peter went down the steps and stood on the path and looked up at me.

'Well, I suppose we'll be seeing you later,' said Con.

'Out,' I said.

'We are out,' said Peter.

I began to go down the steps.

'Mind you don't catch cold,' said Con.

They both laughed.

'I hope she's got understanding neighbours,' said Peter.

They went down the path and got into the Jag.

'See you when you've got your trousers on,' said Con.

I went into the hall and closed the door behind me. There was a pay phone on the wall next to the hall stand. I went over to the phone and picked up the receiver. I dialled 'O'. After a while the operator came on. I asked for a London number. Transfer charge. I waited.

'A Mr Carter is calling from – 3950. Will you pay for the call?'

'Yes, thank you,' said Gerald's voice.

'Go ahead please caller,' said the operator.

'Gerald?' I said.

'Hello, Jack.'

'I've just seen Peter the Dutchman and Con McCarty.'

'Oh yes? How are they?'

'Very well,' I said. 'Providing they keep out of my way.'

'Now look, Jack…'

'No. You look. You look,' I shouted. 'Get off my fucking back, Gerald, or there'll be trouble. I'm telling you.'

'You're telling me, Jack?'

'That's right.'

'Oh, I must have got it wrong: I thought I was the boss and that you worked for me.'

I heard Les's voice in the background saying 'Let me talk to the cunt'. There was a rattle at the other end of the line. Les came on.

183

'Now listen here, cunt,' he said. 'You work for us. You do as you're told. That's what you're paid to do. Either you come back today or you're dead. I mean that.'

'Oh yes?' I said. 'That's very interesting.'

Gerald came back on the line.

'Les didn't mean that Jack,' he said. 'He's very angry just at the moment.'

I heard Les's voice in the background saying yes he fucking well did mean it.

'Then what did he mean?'

'Look, Jack, why don't you come home and save everybody a lot of trouble.'

'I am home. And who's everybody?'

'You, for a start.'

'And?'

'Us.'

'Why?'

'Never mind.'

'You know something, don't you?'

'No, I don't Jack. Just come home with Con and Peter and let's forget it, eh?'

'I'm not coming back, Gerald. Not until I've found out who killed Frank.'

'You know we've asked Con and Peter to bring you back even if you don't particularly want to come?'

'I did gather that,' I said. 'Have they got shooters?'

'Jack...'

'Because they'll bloody well need them,' I said and slammed the phone down.

184

I went up the stairs. My landlady was standing at the top. I walked past her into my room and went over to the window. I looked out. Peter the Dutchman was sitting on the bonnet of the car, smoking, looking up at the window. He waved when he saw me. I couldn't see any sign of Con. He was probably round the back. I turned away and began to get dressed. My landlady came into the room.

'I want you to do something for me,' I said, tying my tie.

'What, and get myself beaten up again?'

'There's no chance of that,' I said.

'Not much.'

'They're friends of mine.'

'That'll make me feel better, will it?'

I ignored her and packed my hold-all and picked up the shotgun. I went out of the room. She followed me downstairs and into the kitchen. I looked over the top of the lace curtains that covered the glass panel in the back door. I couldn't see anything of Con. There were just dustbins and damp grey grass and beyond the thin rain more houses.

'We're going into the garage by the door at the side,' I said. 'I'm going to get in the car and the minute I start it up, I want you to open the garage door. Sharpish.'

'What are you going to do?'

'Sit in the car and whistle *Rule Britannia*.'

I opened the door and stepped outside.

185

My landlady folded her arms and stayed where she was. I leant back and grabbed an arm and pulled her after me.

'Will you be coming back?' she said.

I pushed her into the space between the house and the garage and opened the side door.

'Eh?' she said.

I pushed her inside. I put the shotgun and the hold-all in the boot and got in the car and softly closed the door. I looked at my landlady. She was still standing by the door. She'd folded her arms again. I got out of the car and walked round to her.

'You're not, are you?' she said.

I gave her a clout and shoved her over to the big door and went and got back in the car.

I looked at her and she looked at me. I switched the engine on. She didn't do anything. I waved my arms about at her. She pulled a face at me. I started to get out of the car. She bent down and put her hand on the handle in the middle of the big door. I sat back and nodded to her. She turned the handle. I pressed the starter and the engine caught first time. She pushed against the garage door and it slid upwards. I put my foot down and the car began to move forward.

Peter the Dutchman was still sitting on the bonnet of his Jag. It was still parked across the road from the boarding house. As the door clanged upwards his head turned slowly round so that he was facing the garage. He found himself looking into my eyes. My car picked up speed. It wasn't going fast but it was going fast enough for what I wanted to do. I kept it going straight for the Jag. Straight for where Peter the Dutchman was dangling his legs over the edge of the bonnet. He didn't move. He was still staring into my eyes. I kept on going straight right up until the last second and then I wrenched the steering wheel hard over. The car drifted broadside on to the Jag. The back of my car began to gain momentum. Peter the Dutchman moved. Backwards over the bonnet. His legs up in the air, his cigarette still in his mouth. I pulled the steering wheel back again and straightened the car up. At the same time, I pulled the handbrake on and immediately let it out again. The boot of my car waltzed into the side of the Jag and waltzed back again into the straight. I'd hit the Jag between the bumper and the front wheel. I took off up the road and looked in the mirror. Peter's pride and joy didn't look quite so pretty any more. Neither did Peter. He'd rolled off the bonnet and was on all fours in front of the radiator getting the knees of his twills dirty. He wasn't looking at me as I receded up the road; he was looking at what I'd done to his nice red Jag.

Con had run out of an alley near the boarding house when he'd heard the noise. Now he'd slowed down and was strolling across the road towards Peter the Dutchman and the red Jag. Con was looking up the road in my direction. He was still looking when I turned the corner.

I did a square circuit finishing up in the High Street. I turned right into Clifton Road. On my right was the back of United's main stand. Between me and it was the ground's car park. I pulled over and trundled the car across to the far corner of the car park and stopped under the shadow of a solitary tree that bent over a garden wall at the back of what were once a row of private houses that now had shop fronts facing on to the High Street.

I got out of the car and locked it. I walked back across the car park and turned left and left again back into the High Street. Damp women bundled shopping bags and prams up and down the pavement. Schoolgirls in jeans and anoraks danced in and out of record shops. Television test cards added their own greyness to the grey day. Cyclists traced greasy lines up and down the tarmac.

I bought the *Express* and went into the Kardomah. I got a cup of tea and sat down in a booth at the back. I looked at my watch. It was half-past nine.

At twenty-five past ten I left the Kardomah. At twenty-five to eleven I was walking through the front doors of 'The Cecil'. I was the first in. The barman who served me when I came in with Keith came over. I ordered a large scotch and I asked him what time Keith was on that day. He told me he was supposed to be on the morning session but he hadn't turned up yet. I asked him if he'd got Keith's address. He had. He gave it to me. He kept the change.

I knocked on the door of 27 Priory Street. It was part of a row of bay windowed terraced houses with three-foot gardens. The dust-bins were next to the front door, inside the porch.

The door opened. A man in a cardigan was looking at me.

'Yes?' he said.

'Keith in?' I said.

He turned back into the small hall and stood at the bottom of the stairs.

'Keith,' he shouted. 'Somebody to see you.'

There was no reply.

'Keith?'

There was a reply but there was no way of telling what the words were.

'Sounds as if he had too much last night,' I said.

'Keith?' the man shouted.

'Shall I go up?' I said. 'I've come from the pub to fetch him. He's wanted.'

'Better had,' said the man.

I went up the narrow stairs. I stood on the landing.

'Keith?' I said.

Silence.

'Keith?'

I opened a door.

The room was very small. The curtains were drawn. A big double bed took up nearly all the space. Keith was lying face down on the bed. He was wearing the clothes he'd had on last night. He still had his shoes on. The back of his jacket was torn. I couldn't see his face.

'Keith?' I said.

There was a silence before he answered.

'Bloody well fuck off,' he said. His voice was soft against the eiderdown.

'What happened?' I said.

Nothing.

'Eh?' I said.

Keith moved. It took him a long time, but he moved. He managed to turn himself on to his side and lean on his elbow.

'What you knew would happen,' he said.

'They beat you up,' I said, although I didn't know why.

He didn't say anything. I looked at his face. They'd marked him very well. They'd

190

made a point of it. They'd done a proper job on it.

'You knew they'd come back didn't you?'

When he spoke he moved his lips as little as possible. Too much movement would have been too painful. He talked like a bad ventriloquist.

'No,' I said. 'I didn't.'

Keith tried to give an ironic sneer.

'What did you come for? Professional curiosity?'

'I came to square things up,' I said.

'Oh yes?' he said. 'How?'

'I owe you some money.'

'No,' he said. 'No, you don't.'

I took a lot of money out of my wallet and put it on the bed.

'I don't want it,' he said.

'Yes you do,' I said.

'No, I don't,' he said.

'All right,' I said. 'You don't want it. But I'm leaving it there anyway. You'll be glad of it in three weeks time when your face is back to normal. You'll be glad of all the things you'll be able to buy with it. You might even feel grateful.'

He tried to kick the notes off the bed but he was too stiff. Just a few of them floated down on to the lino.

I turned away and began to go through the door.

'My fiancée's coming tomorrow afternoon,' he said. 'All the way from Liverpool. Nice surprise, isn't it?'

I closed the door and went down the stairs.

'Keith won't be in this morning,' I said to the barman who'd told me where Keith lived. 'You'd better tell the boss.'

'What's up with him?' said the barman.

'Stomach trouble,' I said. 'Very bad.'

I picked up my large scotch and went and sat at one of the tables under the window to wait for Margaret.

Ten minutes later, Con McCarty and Peter the Dutchman walked in.

They looked round and about and finally saw me. They came over.

I realised I wouldn't be getting a Christmas card from Peter this year. Con was his usual smiling self.

'I'll fucking do you for that,' said Peter. 'You're really going to know you've done something.'

'Mean of you, Jack,' said Con. 'Very mean.'

I took a drink of my scotch and said nothing.

'Well?' said Peter.

'Well what?' I said.

'Are you coming?'

I laughed.

'No, I'm bloody not,' I said.

Peter looked at Con. Con was smiling at me.

'So where do you go from there?' I said.

Peter said nothing.

'You're not going to try and take me? Here? Those barmen'd be over here pulling us from together before you could say Eric Robinson. And they know me and they don't know you. You'll just have to wait till I'm elsewhere, won't you?'

Peter looked like midnight in Brixton. Con said:

'Well, we may as well have one as we're here. You don't mind if we join you?'

'Make yourselves at home,' I said.

Con went over to the bar and got two halves of bitter. Peter stayed standing up till Con came back. Con put the beer on the table and sat down. Peter waited a few more seconds before he did the same.

Con drank.

'So how's it going?' he said. 'How's your luck?'

I said nothing.

'Somebody must be worried or else we wouldn't be here,' he said.

I said nothing again.

'All right,' said Con. 'Who's going to win this afternoon? Spurs or Arsenal?'

'Spurs,' I said.

We both smiled.

Con took another drink.

'Saw Audrey last night,' he said.

'Oh yes?' I said.

'Yes,' he said. 'Asked me if I'd heard anything.'

'And?'

'I hadn't heard anything.'

'They say she's a good screw,' said Peter, looking at me.

'Oh?' I said.

'Yes,' said Peter. 'Jokey Jim was saying so.'

'He'd know would he?'

Peter shrugged.

'Why should he bother to tell you, poof-dah?' I said.

I thought Peter was going to get up but he didn't because he thought about it first.

'Incidentally,' Con said to Peter, 'I expect you know Stone Ginger's back at the Swiss?'

'I knew it,' said Peter.

'Just thought I'd mention it. Apparently he's not feeling friendly towards you at present.'

'I knew that too.'

'You could always kiss and make up,' I said. 'Or do you make up before you kiss?'

'Be funny,' said Peter. 'Enjoy it. There's always later.'

Con finished his beer.

'Another?' he said.

He picked up the glasses. I put a pound on the table.

'It's my shout,' I said.

Con shrugged and picked up the money and left me and Peter looking at each other.

The doors opened and Margaret came in. She was wearing dark glasses and her green coat. She couldn't see me at first but she didn't take her glasses off. When she saw where I was sitting she pushed her hands in her coat pockets and ambled over on her shaky heels. Con got back with the drinks at the same time as Margaret reached the table.

She looked at us all.

'Margaret,' I said, 'meet two old friends of mine from the smoke. Peter and Con. Margaret.'

Con put the drinks down and shook hands. Peter nodded.

'What are you having, Margaret?' I said.

Margaret was having a vodka and lime. She was also having second thoughts about being there. Peter and Con had got her worried. All sorts of thoughts were going on behind the dark glasses.

I pulled a chair away from the table. She sat down. I went and got her a vodka and lime. When I got back Con was doing the talking.

'Lived here all your life, have you?' he was saying.

''cepting a year, yeah,' she said.

'Fellers,' I said. 'You wouldn't mind, would you, but me and Margaret have a few things to discuss. Frank's affairs and that...'

Con stood up.

'No, of course not,' he said. 'We'll wait for you at the bar.'

Peter stood up but not so quickly.

'See you later,' I said.

Peter looked at me and then he and Con picked up their drinks and went over to the bar and sat on a couple of stools. I sat down next to Margaret.

'Glad you could make it,' I said.

She had a drink.

'Who are them fellers?' she said.

'Them? Just some blokes I know from London.'

'What are they doing up here?'

'Dunno,' I said. 'Maybe they're on their holidays.'

'Funny,' she said.

'Why?' I said. 'Do they bother you?'

'Why should they?'

I shrugged.

'No reason.'

'Well they don't.'

I took my fags out and gave her one. Lighting us up, I said:

'Doreen was saying she could stay with the parents of some friends of hers. More or less indefinitely, like. Know anything of them?'

She inhaled.

'She's a friend called Yvonne. 'spect it's her.'

196

'Know what her folks are like?'

'Her dad's a bus inspector. They live up Wilton Estate.'

'Reckon she's telling the truth? About being able to stay as long as she likes?'

'Don't see why not. She's always having her tea round there and staying nights and that.'

'So you think she'd be all right with them?'

'They'd look after her. They're like that.'

'Because I told her she could come away with me if she wanted.'

'What did she say to that?'

'Not much.'

She took another drink.

'How did she seem, all in all?' she said.

'She's not as bad as she might be. But I should think that's because she's a little tougher than most.'

Margaret didn't answer.

'Will you keep seeing her?' I said.

'I should think so.'

I took a drink.

'How are you feeling about it all?' I said.

She shrugged.

'I expect it was a bit of a shock,' I said.

'Yes,' she said.

'Especially Frank being the sort of bloke he was,' I said.

Inhaling, she nodded.

'You don't know of anything that might have been worrying him? You know, getting

197

him down one way or another?'

'How do you mean?'

'Well, you know, something on his mind big enough for him to go out and tank up on scotch in order to sort it out. Or to forget about it.'

She shook her head.

'Nothing?' I said. 'Nothing at all?'

'Why should there be anything?'

'Just funny that it happened that way of all ways,' I said.

'One way's the same as another,' she said. 'Makes no difference in the end. Makes no difference to Frank, does it?'

'It might make a difference to me.'

There was a pause that some people mightn't have noticed before she said:

'How do you mean?'

I changed course.

'How did you feel about him?'

'He was all right to me,' she said.

'Nothing more?' I said. 'Just another feller?'

'He was nicer than most.'

'But he was still just another feller, wasn't he?'

'Yes.'

'Even though he was nicer than most?'

'Yes.'

I didn't say anything to that.

'Well I can't help the way I am,' she said.

'Why did you see him so regular?'

'Only once a week.'

'I'd call that regular.'

'Well it was a change. He was gentlemanly. I liked that.'

'So long as it was once a week.'

'Look, I'm me, right? You're not. We're what we are, like it or not.'

'And you being what you are enjoyed the Big Night of the week out with a bloke like Frank?'

'He liked me. It makes a difference.'

'Why?'

'Why what?'

'Why did he like you?'

Red spots jumped to her cheeks.

'I don't know,' she said.

'Are you sure "like's" the right word?'

She didn't answer.

'I expect you know he never got owt from his missus,' I said. 'A bloke like Frank'd never admit to himself that it'd worry him. He'd pretend it didn't matter. But if somebody like you made it easily available he just might twist himself into believing that he liked you for what you were and not for what you'd got.'

She didn't answer.

'So that'd make him just like the rest of them, wouldn't it?'

'Yes,' she said between compressed lips. 'Yes, I suppose it would. But if he'd convinced himself then maybe it wasn't too hard to convince me. And that works out like what I said, doesn't it?'

I looked over to the bar. Con and Peter were talking and drinking, occasionally looking across to see what I was doing.

'Anyway,' she said. 'What is this? Flaming *Dragnet?* Why all the bloody needle?'

'Look,' I said, 'I'll ask you again: You don't know of anything, anything at all that Frank might have been worrying about. Any trouble he might have been in? Anybody he was frightened of?'

'What are you talking about?'

'Come on, Margaret,' I said. 'Do you really think that Frank just filled himself up with scotch so that he couldn't see and accidentally drove off top road?'

'What do you mean? That's what happened?'

'If he did that it was for a reason. And I'd like to know the reason.'

'You mean he might have done it on purpose?'

I said yes. I wanted to see what she'd say if she thought I felt it was suicide. She thought a lot about things before she said anything.

'You won't like this,' she said. 'But it's the only thing I can think of.'

'What is it?' I said.

'Friday night, the Friday before the Sunday he was killed, there was trouble. See, Frank'd been asking me to leave Dave, me

200

husband. He wanted me to go and live with him. Get a divorce. Even if I'd wanted to I wouldn't have. Dave would have killed us both. But Frank was always asking. He was asking Friday night. I said "no" for the umpteenth time and he turned nasty. There was a scene. I left the pub. Frank came out in street after me. I told him to leave me alone but he kept following me. He followed me all the way home. He'd had a few. I went in but he wouldn't go away. He kicked up stink in street for about half an hour before he buggered off. Dave wasn't home but he heard about it next day. We've got nice neighbours round our way. He gave me one of his good hidings and in due course asked me who the feller was. Well, I wouldn't tell him because he would have killed Frank. And I didn't want Doreen involved. So I said, "Look, if I promise to stop at home and never look at another feller, would he leave it at that?" I'd never said that before and he was so surprised he said yes. So Sunday morning I went round to tell Frank I wasn't seeing him any more. Doreen wasn't there. He went mad. He did everything. He crawled, he threatened me, he said he'd do anything. When he saw it wasn't any good he said if I didn't go with him, he'd kill himself. He said he meant it. 'Course I didn't believe him. I just thought he was going on. But after what happened on Sunday … I mean, whether he meant it or not, it looks as though that's why he went out on the scotch.'

I didn't say anything.

'I wasn't going to tell you,' she said. 'I was frightened what you might do. But I reckon you've a right to know.'

I finished my drink.

Now what she'd just told me was very interesting. Because if Frank'd wanted Margaret to leave her husband he'd have asked her just the once and if she'd said no, he would never have mentioned it again. Likewise, if she'd gone to tell him they were washed up he wouldn't have argued about it. He'd let her do what she wanted to do, what ever he felt about it. Frank didn't like people seeing inside him.

So assuming my feelings about my own brother were true, what she'd just told me wasn't. It was a pack of lies. And if she'd told me a pack of lies there was a good reason for it. Probably just the reason I was looking for. But I wasn't going to find it sitting in 'The Cecil' with Con McCarty and Peter the Dutchman and half a dozen barmen for an audience. So I said:

'So that's it then. I was right.'

She didn't say anything.

'It doesn't make me very happy, Margaret, but it's best you've told me. It's a thing I'd got to know.'

She finished her drink.

'Let me get you another,' I said.

'Thanks,' she said.

I stood up. Con and Peter slid off their seats the minute I moved but they slid back again when they saw I was approaching the bar.

'Making progress?' said Con.

I smiled.

'What is she? Business or pleasure?'

'That's something for you to decide,' I said.

I ordered large ones and took them back to the table. She'd already started another cigarette.

'Well,' I said, 'you needn't worry. I'm not going to mark you. What happened couldn't be helped. Things just worked out a certain way. Nothing I can do will make any difference.'

She didn't say anything.

'Let's drink to it,' I said.

She raised her glass.

'No,' I said. 'I've a better idea: let's drink to Frank.'

The glass remained where it had been before I'd spoken, about an inch from her lips.

'To Frank,' I said. 'Wherever he is.'

'Frank,' she said.

We drank.

I put my glass down and looked across at

Con and Peter. Con was getting some more drinks in.

'You'll have to excuse us now, Margaret,' I said. 'I've got a bit of business to discuss.'

She drank up and stood up.

'Well,' she said. 'I don't suppose I'll be seeing you again.'

'I don't suppose you will,' I said.

She turned away.

'Thanks again for making the arrangements,' I said.

She turned back and looked at me. I was amazed to see that tears were pouring from behind the dark glasses. She kept on looking at me for a few seconds then she turned away again and walked out of the pub.

I wondered what had brought that on but I didn't have any time to think about it what with Con and Peter watching me like hawks.

I walked over to them again.

'Must have been business,' said Con, noting Margaret's departure. 'Having one, Jack?'

I nodded.

Con got me a drink. He twisted round on his stool to reach for it for me. He was in a very awkward position. Peter was draining his glass. So I punched Con in the kidneys and gave Peter a backhander in his guts and turned and ran as fast as I could down the aisle between the bar and the tables. When I got to the end of the row I pulled over a couple of tables just in case but Con and Peter were only just beginning to come after me. If you're only Number Two you should try harder. I whipped through the Gent's door and opened the door that led into the car park. I began to run down the short flight of steps.

The trouble was there was a man standing at the top of the steps and his leg was stretched out in front of me.

I didn't touch a step. I made sure I landed O.K. and began rolling out of the impact but that didn't do me much good because at the bottom of the steps there was another man who began kicking at me even before I hit the floor. I managed to get an anklehold on him and twist him over but not before he'd given me a few handy ones in my ribs and in the small of my back. But at the same time as he went over the man who'd been standing at the top of the steps was now on the tarmac and he began the whole process all over again. I went back on my shoulders and gave him a double legged kick in the flies. He went green and spewy. I was getting up as Con and Peter came boiling down the steps. Con had his knife out. He was smiling broader than at any other time during that day. The first bloke I'd put down was already back on his feet. The other local boy was dragging himself along on his stomach trying to forget he was alive.

I was running even before I was upright. Not that I held out much hope of out distancing them after the good footwork that'd been put in but it was the only thing I could do under the circumstances.

'Not looking for that one, were you, Jack?' Con shouted as he came after me across the car park.

I kept on going but they were closing and I knew they weren't trying all that hard.

Then I became aware of a white TR4 accelerating towards me from the direction of the far exit of the car park. It had me dead between the headlights.

Christ, I thought, the bastards've thought of it all.

I stopped running. The car got closer and so did the boys. I tensed up, getting ready to try and jump to one side, like a goalie weighing up a bloke approaching a ball on the penalty spot.

But before I had time to jump the car swerved past me and carried on towards the boys. They began to slow down. The driver threw a lock on the wheel. The car went into a four wheel drift, broadside on to the boys. Boys began to leap in all directions. Peter got some more marks on his twills. Con's knife flew up in the air, bright against the grey wet sky. Beyond the knife, I noticed a bevy of white-shirted barmen perched on the car park steps, gaping at the scene.

The car went into opposite lock and zoomed back in my direction. The driver threw the brakes on. The car skidded alongside me. The driver stretched behind the wheel and the passenger door flew open. The driver was a girl.

I bundled in, remembering why it was I knew her. 'The Casino'. The girl with the giggles. The one who was drunk.

She still was.

The car leapt forward. I looked out of the back. Con and the others were scuttling in the opposite direction making for the red Jag.

We swung out of the car park. The girl was grinning all over her face but her eyes were foggy and dull.

I couldn't really think of anything to say that could follow the scene that had just happened so I waited for her. She wouldn't be able to keep quiet for long.

We zig-zagged up and down a few streets. There was no sign of the red Jag.

I took my fags out. They were all bent up. I stuck one in my mouth and lit up.

'You didn't know you had a fairy God-mother did you?' she said.

'No,' I said. 'I didn't.'

'A fairy God-mother all of your own. Aren't you lucky?'

'Yes, I am.'

We skidded round another corner.

'Where are we going?' I said.

'To the fairy God-mother's castle, of course.'

'Oh.'

'To see the Demon King.'

'Kinnear?'

She laughed.

'If I said yes, you'd get out, wouldn't you?'

'I'm not sure,' I said.

We began to slow down.

'How did you happen to know where I'd be?'

'The Demon King wanted to talk to you. So he phoned up a few places and you were at one of them. He waved his wand and I was despatched to bring you to him. I was going to park the pumpkin but you saved me the trouble. Lucky for you I was held up in the traffic.'

'Lucky for me you're drunk or else you wouldn't have been able to drive like that.'

'Nasty,' she said.

'He must have been pretty sure I'd want to see him if he sent you.'

'Oh, he was. He told me something to tell you that would make you come. Like a magic spell.'

'And what did he tell you to tell me?'

'We're there now,' she said. 'You'll have to wait and see. That's for being nasty.'

The car stopped. We got out. She was

drunk enough to leave her keys in the dash-board. That might be a nice thing to know later on.

We were in the middle of a dozen blocks of tall council flats. They looked greyer than the day. We walked across a dull wet patch of grass and under one of the blocks and turned left. There was a lift, one of those aluminium finish things that always smell of piss. We got in. She pressed Four on the panel. She pushed her hands in to the pockets of her short artificial fur coat and leaned her back against the wall and looked at me. The door rattled shut and the lift moved. I threw my cigarette on the floor; the stink didn't improve the flavour. The girl kept looking at me.

The lift stopped and the doors opened.

We got out and walked along the balcony. She stopped and took a key out of her pocket and put it in a lock and opened a door. I went through.

I stood in the small hall and waited for her to close the door. She closed it and walked past me and opened another one. She looked at me. I went through the door.

It wasn't a big room but it was very nicely done out. Low tables, divans, coloured cushions, white walls, a little bit of stripped pine, the occasional big modern picture, the odd bits of copper. Nice.

Cliff Brumby was sitting on one of the low

divans. He was wearing the beautiful overcoat of the previous night. Underneath he had on a white silk rollneck and a bright red cardigan. He was sitting with one arm draped along the back of the divan. His other arm was placed elegantly across the lower part of his stomach and between the fingers of his hand was a freshly lit cigarette.

'Hello, Jack,' he said.

I looked at him.

'Make yourself at home,' he said. 'Only not like last night, eh?'

I sat down and said nothing. The girl went over to an open cocktail cabinet and looked at me as she picked out three glasses with one hand and a bottle of scotch with another. Then she set them down on the low table that was between me and Cliff and went out of the room. She came back with a jug of water and came my side of the table and leant over the table and poured the drinks. As she poured, she swayed, allowing me to see right up to the maker's name. Cliff saw me looking.

'Glenda,' he said, 'your fanny's in Jack's face.'

Still leaning over, Glenda screwed her head round to look at me.

'I don't see him complaining,' she said.

'He's seen it before,' said Brumby. 'Get yourself round this side.'

She straightened up and walked round the

table and flopped on the divan next to Brumby. She undid her coat and planted her feet on the table. One leg was bent and the other was fully extended. I was being given another treat. Brumby gave her a long look. Eventually she took her feet off the table but with the way she was sitting it didn't really matter. It also didn't really matter because most of the time I'd been watching Brumby's face to see what went.

'Well,' said Brumby, 'you'll be wondering what I've got to say.'

I said nothing.

'Last night after you'd gone, I thought I'd do a little bit of asking about. Seeing as how you weren't exactly forthcoming as to why you should want to see me at half-past two in the morning.'

I lit up.

'Very interesting it was. What I was told, like. About you having a brother and all that. Especially the part about you asking around about as to the likelihood of his being knocked off.'

He leant forward and picked up a glass. 'I got to thinking: wouldn't it be nice if the bloke you were after was a bloke I'd rather like to have off my back? Wouldn't it be a bit of all right if you and me had mutual interests in getting rid of a certain gentleman?'

'Like who?' I said.

211

Brumby took a drink. He thought he'd got me hooked.

'I expect you know all about my line,' he said.

I didn't answer.

'Machines. The arcades,' he said. 'I expect you even know how many I've got and on how many sea fronts.'

I inhaled.

'Nice business. Looks after itself. People put money in the machines. I take it out. Not much rough stuff. Just the occasional friendly persuasion with owners of property I don't own.'

'I know about the business,' I said.

'Believe me,' he said, 'it's a business that's made me very happy. Never really wanted to branch out into anything else. Hard enough getting this little lot set up. Life's too short. I've got what I want and I use it. I appreciate it. I started hawking scrap in a barrow in nineteen forty four, when I was sixteen. I remember where I've come from.'

He took a drink.

'But happy as I've been, no business maintains its status quo. You've got to expand. Otherwise you may as well pack it in. So as far as the arcades are concerned, well, there's only so many without going outside a given area. And I wouldn't want to do that. For more reasons than one. So what's left. The pubs? The breweries make

212

their own arrangements. The clubs? Some belong to owners, but some don't. The constitutionals, the Labours, the working mens. So, quite legitimately, I send representatives round and about. 'Course, lots of places already have got machines. But mine are better: they pay out more often and at the same time they pay out less. The customers like them and so do the management. To my reps it's like selling iced water in the Sahara. They're keen lads. One of them gets a bit too keen. He flogs some machines in a place that's already got machines. Okay. But the manager of this place is very silly. He doesn't tell certain people what he's done. Certain people with interests in the club. There's some trouble. The upshot is I have to eat shit and stop pushing my machines in the clubs. That's bad but I have to take it. I'm not big enough not to. So as far as I'm concerned, that's it. Apparently not. These people I've offended start thinking wouldn't it be nice if all Cliff Brumby's machines and all Cliff Brumby's outlets belonged to us? Once we've got hold of them, a lot of other seaside venues would drop into place. I got to hear all this from a little bird I pay money to hear things for me.'

The girl smiled blankly into her empty glass.

'So I'm very worried. If they want to do

this then they're going to do it and that's all there is to it. I'll be lucky if they let me keep my barrow. I can't fight them. I haven't got that kind of set-up. But I've got to fix them before they fix me. Trouble is if I try and it doesn't come off and they know I've tried, I'm dead, aren't I, Jack?'

I blew smoke into the air.

Cliff reached down beside him and picked up a briefcase and put it on the table and opened it. He took out two bundles of very new banknotes.

'A grand,' he said. 'It belongs to you. Along with a name I'm going to give you.'

'What name?' I said.

'Paice.'

I looked at him.

'Paice did it,' he said, 'and Kinnear would give the say so.'

'Why?' I said.

'I don't know. All I know is what I've been told.'

The girl poured herself another drink.

'I understand there was a bit of a kerfuffle last Saturday night at "The Casino",' he said. 'People shitting bricks all over the place. Especially Eric. Your brother's name was mentioned. Eric goes off with some hard boys. Eric comes back and after that your brother's dead.'

'Why?' I said.

Brumby shrugged.

'I've told you as much as I know,' he said.

I looked at him.

'Yes, well,' I said, 'it's not enough, is it, Cliff?'

I stood up. Brumby looked at me.

'Do me a favour,' I said. 'Do you really expect me to go to Eric or Kinnear and push them over on your say so? You must be joking.'

Brumby carried on looking at me.

'I'll tell you what I think you found out after last night's sniffing; you found out that they put me on to you hoping I'd do you and then it occurred to you it might be a good idea to get me to do the same to them. Stroll on Cliff. You must think I'm bleeding barmy.'

'You're wrong, Jack.'

'Sure,' I said, 'if you say so.'

'Jack...'

'Ta-ra Cliff.'

I walked out of the room. The girl watched me all the way. Or should I say both of me.

I waited in the grey rain for Brumby to leave. The idea was to go back and see Glenda on her own. See what she really knew. And what Cliff really knew. The trouble was it didn't quite work out like that.

I'd been standing there for about quarter of an hour when the red Jag slid up and tucked in behind the TR4. Only this time there was only one person in the car and that was Con.

He didn't get out. He lit up and slid down in his seat and relaxed. He looked very comfy.

I was standing in the entrance to one of the blocks of flats. I realised I'd be invisible to Con behind the steamy plate glass. But that was only temporary. I had to move sometime. And after all, there was only Con. I walked out into the rain.

Con saw me. He eased himself up in his seat a little bit and wound the window down.

'Jack,' he called.

I stood and looked at him.

'Here a minute. I've something to tell you.'

I stayed where I was.

'Your niece,' he said. 'She's been asking for you. Wants to see you.'

I walked over to the car. Con didn't get out.

'Have you done anything to her, Con?'

Con smiled.

'Now, would I?' he said. 'But I had to leave her with Peter, didn't I? You know how Peter feels about the opposite sex.'

'Where are they?'

'Get in and I'll tell you.'

We looked at one another. Con said:

'I've got a shooter in my pocket. But there's no need for that is there?'

I didn't say anything. Con opened the door on the driver's side and slid over into the passenger's seat. I walked round the front of the car and got in.

'There's a lovely boy, Jack,' said Con.

I started the car and sat there.

'Carry on,' said Con.

'I don't know where we're going, do I?'

'I'll tell you when we're moving.'

We pulled away from the kerb.

'Where to?' I said.

'Jackson Street,' he said.

We drove through the empty back streets. As we turned into Jackson Street, Con said:

'I wouldn't have a go, Jack. Remember Peter.'

I began to slow down.

Con had both hands in his pockets. One on the shooter and one on the knife. I stopped the car and pulled the handbrake on. Then I flashed my hand between Con's legs and grabbed his balls and squeezed hard.

Con opened his mouth to scream but before any sound could come out I pulled his hat over his face and stuffed as much of it as I could into his mouth. I let go of his balls and gave him one in the throat. He began to choke so I hit him on the temple with my elbow and pulled the hat out of his mouth. He fell forward and cracked his forehead on the dashboard. With a little bit of assistance from myself.

I took the gun and the knife and put them in my pockets and got out of the car without slamming the door. I crossed the pavement and walked down the passage that led to the back gardens, turned left and ducked down below the kitchen window. Nobody came and opened the back door so I had a quick look through the kitchen window.

The door between the kitchen and the scullery was open. I could see right through.

Doreen was sitting in Frank's chair. Her legs were drawn up underneath her. I couldn't see her face because her hands were covering it. Peter the Dutchman was sitting on the divan, leaning forward. Looking as though he was chatting in a nice friendly manner.

I ducked down, then straightened up and then very, very carefully I opened the back door. I stood there for a minute or two to make sure I hadn't been heard. I hadn't. Peter was still talking.

'Of course,' he was saying, 'there's worse things. I mean, I once saw a snotty little dolly like you given the treatment by a couple of bull-dykes. Nice it was. They like it rough, you know. They like a bit of pain and a bit of blood, some of those bulls. These two did. They had some really good ideas. What they did you see...'

Peter stopped talking. Very abruptly. A shadow had fallen between him and Doreen. Peter did a long slow take until for the second time that day he found himself looking into my eyes.

'What did they do, Peter?' I said.

His eyes were glass. Doreen's hands fell away from her face at the sound of my voice.

'Come on, Ginger Boy,' I said. 'Tell us what they did.'

Peter's mouth opened but no words came out. Things exploded in my head. I fell on Peter, straddling him, pushing him down on to the divan. I punched his face until my fists got slippery. Then I turned him over and gave him some in his kidneys. Doreen watched in a kind of crazy silence.

I stood up and Peter slid off face down on the carpet, one leg still on the divan. I drew my foot back to kick the side of his head. Doreen screamed. I kicked him anyway.

When I'd done that, I took a fag out and lit up and stood there looking down at him. Doreen was looking at him too, but the difference was that she was crying.

I went outside to the car. Con was where I'd left him, trying to lift himself up in his seat. I opened the car door.

'Get out,' I said.

Con tried to get out but he couldn't. I took hold of his coat collar and pulled. He slid out of his seat and on to his knees on the pavement. A couple of kids on bikes drew level, slowed down, then picked up speed again. I hoisted Con to his feet and bundled him into the house.

I got him into the living-room and dumped him on the divan. Then I went into the kitchen and found the washing line. I tipped Con on to the floor next to Peter and trussed them up back to back.

Doreen hadn't moved.

'Right,' I said. 'From now on you stay with me.'

Doreen carried on crying.

'Do you hear?' I said.

'What's going on? What's going on?' she said, shaking her head from side to side.

'Never mind,' I said. 'You'll be well out of it by Monday.'

She carried on shaking her head.

'Come on,' I said.

She didn't get up so I lifted her up out of the chair.

'Look,' I said. 'You're coming with me.'

'No,' she said her body going limp. 'No.'

'All right,' I said. 'It's up to you. But you can't stay here. I'll take you to your friend's place.'

I took hold of her arm and guided her out of the house and put her in the Jag. I got in and pressed the starter.

Wilton Estate was lifeless in the rain. Hedgeless lawns sopped up the wet greyness. I stopped the car.

Doreen was still crying.

'Look, I'm sorry,' I said. 'About them blokes: they're from the smoke. They want me to go back with them, that's all.'

Doreen didn't answer.

'Anyway, I'm chucking London. It'll be all right in South Africa. Sunshine. Modern cities. Not like this hole. You'll like it.'

'I'm not going. Not with you. Me dad wouldn't want me to.'

'Why not?'

She took a handkerchief from her pocket and dabbed at her eyes.

'Because he bloody hated you, that's why.'

'Did he say that?'

'He didn't have to, did he? I could tell. He didn't have to say owt.'

I looked out at the rain.

'I'm not surprised he hated you now I know you. He'd have killed you if he'd been there. Trying to say he was mixed up in summat. Getting on to me about it.'

'You don't know it all,' I said. 'So don't think you do.'

She opened the car door.

'Anyway, I'm not going any-bloody-where with you. So you can stuff that in your pipe and smoke it.'

She got out and slammed the door and

began to walk down the road. I watched her go. Eventually she turned left into one of the crescents. I eased the car forward and stopped at the turning. Doreen was about halfway up the crescent when she left the footpath and walked across the green towards one of the houses. She didn't look back. I waited till she was out of sight then backed up into the crescent and pointed the car back in the direction of the High Street.

I drove the Jag into United's car park. It was three quarters full. An attendant was standing about wearing one of those tent-shaped rubberized coats. I stopped and pushed a half crown piece out of the window. He gave me a ticket and I drove over to the far corner where I'd left the hired car. I parked the Jag nearby and got out and locked it up. I looked over to where the attendant was. He was walking away from me, towards his box. The crowd's roar ebbed and flowed across the wet sky. I ducked down and took out Con's knife and did the tyres on the Jag. It didn't take long. Con prided himself on his knife. Then I got into the hired car and drove off the car park. The attendant gawped into the car as I drove past his box.

The TR4 was still outside the flats. I drove the car round the corner of the flats and parked by the adjoining garage, got out and crossed over. There was no way of knowing whether Brumby was still there or not but I'd worry about that after I'd rung the doorbell.

The flats were as deserted as before. I went up in the lift. Nobody was on the balcony.

I rang the bell and waited. I could hear bathtaps running.

After I'd rung the bell a dozen times and waited nearly five minutes the door opened.

She still had her coat on and she was still drunk.

'I thought maybe I'd come back,' I said.

She stared at me. At least as much as her drooping eyelids and her glassy eyes would let her. Then she smiled and did the tongue and teeth bit.

'What for?' she said.

I said nothing.

'You can't come in unless you tell me,' she said.

'I thought maybe you'd be able to guess.'

She shook her head still giving me the stare, the tongue and the teeth.

'No,' she said, 'I'm no good at guessing games.'

'Actually,' I said, 'it's gone clean out of me head. Funny, isn't it. Still, it might come back if you ask me in.'

She'd been holding her coat together at the neck. She took her hand away and the coat fell open. She must have been getting ready for the bath when I'd rung the bell because she didn't have her dress on, only a black half slip and underneath that I imagined she was wearing what I'd already been treated to a view of.

'That helps,' I said. 'But I still can't quite tie it down.'

She giggled.

'Come in,' she said. 'I'll tie it down for you. If you like that kind of thing.'

I went through the hall and into the lounge. Glenda disappeared for a minute and I heard the bathtaps being turned off. I sat down on the divan where Brumby had sat earlier. The glasses were still there where they'd been left. So was the bottle. I poured some into my glass and drank it and then poured some more and took a fag out and lit up.

Glenda floated into the room. She'd got rid of the coat. Instead of coming and sitting next to me on the divan she stood on the other side of the low table and poured herself a very big drink and then sat down where I'd sat earlier and put her stockinged feet up on the table.

'This is where I came in,' I said.

'That's right,' she said. 'Just refreshing your memory.'

She manoeuvred the glass up to her mouth and drank until some of the whisky began to trickle down her chin. She put the glass down and re-focussed on me. When she'd managed that, I leant across and offered her a fag. She took it and dropped it so she had to shift her legs off the table in order to bend down and pick the fag up off the floor. She got it into her mouth and I lit her up and I sat back and she sat back and blew smoke all over and looked at me and said:

'Well?'

'Well what?'

She gave me what she imagined was a knowing look.

'I see,' she said, 'I see.'

'You see what?'

'You're enjoying things the way they are, are you? Me like this and you like that?'

I smiled.

'Let's just say I like a slow build-up. If there's time, that is.'

'Time?'

'Cliff. He might be coming back.'

She shook her head.

'He's at match, isn't he? In his reserved seat two rows behind the bloody Lord Mayor. He'll learn one day.'

'Learn what?'

'Learn to stop playing silly buggers. He's off his bloody head. Thinks he's going to be another Kinnear.' She giggled. 'He might be getting somewhere the day the Lord Mayor owes him money instead of Kinnear.'

'How is it you're on the eyeball for Cliff then?'

'He pays money.'

'So does Kinnear.'

'Only if I work for it.'

'Doesn't he pay you enough, then?'

'Sometimes. When he wants a performance at one of his parties. Or when there's a Blue on.'

'Aren't you frightened what Kinnear would do to you if he found out?'

'He won't.'

'How do you know?'

'Because he thinks I'm simple. He wouldn't give me credit, would he?'

'He could still find out, accidental.'

'How? Nobody knows about this place. Cliff pays for it and I only come here to see Cliff.'

She took a drink. I decided it was time.

'Incidentally,' I said. 'The other night. When I came to "The Casino". Did, er, did Kinnear say anything? After I'd gone?'

She laughed.

'What do you think?'

'Yes, I know, but, like, what did he say? Because what Cliff was saying earlier, about Kinnear having my brother done, if it was true, well, maybe something was said.'

She looked at me. Her eyes were focussing very well right now.

'I thought you didn't believe Cliff?'

'I didn't, but I got thinking. Maybe it'd be as well to check up.'

'Through me?'

'I just thought, well, as you weren't particularly interested about where the money came from, maybe you wouldn't mind some from me, either.'

I took my wallet out and put it on the table. She looked at it.

'This is why you came back is it?'

'Not entirely, no.'

'You're sure about that, are you?'

I smiled.

'Yes, I'm sure.'

It was her turn to smile again.

'Well, you'll have to prove it, won't you?'

'What do you mean?'

'Come over here and I'll show you.'

She leant back on the divan and pulled her legs up to her titties and clasped them to her but almost immediately she had to let go with one of her hands to stop her falling over sideways.

'Then what?' I said.

'Then I'll tell you.'

'Why not tell me now?'

She shook her head.

'I could beat it out of you.'

She shook her head again.

'Why not?' I said.

'I'd lie.'

227

'You could lie anyway.'

'Why should I? I might be doing myself a favour.'

'How?'

She got up from where she was sitting and made her way round the table and sat down next to me.

'What's the matter?' she said. 'Aren't you in the mood?'

She smelt of nylon and sweet body-sweat.

'Is that it? Do you want putting in the mood?'

She put her hand on my stomach and slithered one of her legs across me. I felt her mouth against my ear and she stared to lick round it .

'Come on,' she said. 'Glenda'll tell you. After.'

She began to un-zip my flies. I decided to let her have it her way. I put my arm round her and pulled her down on to me and let her get on with what she wanted to do. After a few minutes she looked up and said:

'You're not trying.'

'Get on with it,' I said.

She did but it wasn't any good. I couldn't do very much about it. I stood up.

'Let's forget it, eh?' I said.

She struggled to her feet.

'I know,' she said. 'I know what we can do.'

'Look…'

She took hold of my hand and began to

pull me towards the door.

'Come on,' she said. 'Don't forget, Glenda won't tell if you're not a good boy.'

I picked up my glass and let her tug me out of the lounge and through the hall and into the bedroom. It was as nicely done out as the lounge.

There was a big double bed with a red silk counterpane. The carpet was wall-to-wall and deep orange. A long mirror took up half of one wall and there was another the width of the bed disappearing behind the pillows. Above this mirror there was a deep shelf about two foot wide. On the shelf there was an eight mil. film projector.

Glenda let go of my hand and climbed on the bed and wobbled about finally steadying herself by hanging on to the shelf. When she was fairly sure of her balance she released one of her hands and switched on the projector. The projector was loaded with a two hundred foot spool. The leader had already been threaded through and fixed into the take-up spool.

All that happened was that the light came on and lit up the blank wall opposite the bed.

'Do you always provide such a comprehensive service?'

She giggled.

'Cliff wanted to see one,' she said. 'So I sort of got hold of this.'

She frowned at the brilliant square of light on the wall.

'It's not working. Why isn't the sod working?'

'Look,' I said. 'I've seen them. Too many. I used to flog them to the punters. They don't...'

'Oh, this is different,' she said. 'I'm in it. You'll like it.'

She turned back to the projector.

'But why isn't the sod working?'

I took a drink and sank down on the edge of the bed.

'Try pushing the switch to the next stop,' I said.

She pushed the switch to the next stop. The motor started to whirr and the spools began to roll. Blank leader flowed on the white wall. Glenda flopped down full length on to the bed. Then the titles appeared. They'd been pencilled on a piece of card and held up to the camera by somebody with the shakes.

The titles said: *Schoolgirl Wanks.*

The titles went on for a long time. I started to get up.

'Look, it's no good. I...'

'Watch,' she said, taking my glass.

The titles had stopped. Now on the wall there was a bedroom and in the bedroom was Glenda, dressed as a schoolgirl, sitting at a dressing table combing her hair. She did this for a few minutes and then picked up a framed photograph and held it to her bosom and closed her eyes. Then she put the photograph back in its place and stood up and started to change into her normal clothes, spraying perfume all over her and generally tarting herself up.

The scene changed. Now there was a room with a settee in it, flush to the wall. Sitting on the settee, thumbing through a magazine there was a girl. She was very pretty. She had long blonde hair parted in the middle and it was so soft and fine that the girl had to keep pushing it back from her face. She was wearing a gym-slip and white socks. To one side of the settee there was a grate with no fire in it. To the other side of the settee there was a T.V. set. There was lino on the floor and an aluminium garden chair intruded in one corner of the frame. There was a little clock on the mantelpiece above the grate. The hands were at ten to four. Adjacent to the settee, just to one side of the girl, there was a low stool and on the stool was a tray with cups and a tea pot. The girl leant forward and picked up a cup and mimed sipping and put the cup back and then went on thumbing through the magazine.

I recognised both the room and the girl. The room was Albert Swift's kitchen. The girl was Doreen.

I turned to look at Glenda. Her mouth was open and her lids were even heavier and slow breath rasped in her throat. In ten seconds she would be asleep.

The film carried on running through the projector. I let it.

The film cut and now the camera was looking over her shoulder as she, Frank's daughter (or mine) turned the pages of the magazine on her lap.

She stopped at a particular page. The camera shakily zoomed in on a picture of Englebert Humperdinck. The camera cut back to the original shot of Doreen on the settee.

She lifted up the magazine and kissed the photograph and closed her eyes.

Then she propped up the magazine against one of the arms of the settee and with her feet still on the floor she moved sideways so that her elbows rested on the cushions of the settee and her chin rested in her hands as she stared at the photograph in the magazine. Eventually after a certain amount of writhing, she began to massage her breasts. After she'd done that for a while her hand slid down along her body and she began to squeeze the material of her dress in the area between her legs. When she'd finished doing that she began to pull at the hem of her dress. But before she could do that an exterior shot was cut in. A car drew up and a man got out and the man was Albert. He was wearing a false moustache.

The film cut back to Albert's kitchen. Doreen acted out hearing the car and sitting up quick and pulling herself together. The door opened. Albert came in. His lips moved. Doreen got up from the settee and the camera panned and followed her past Albert and over to the door. She stuck her head round it and acted out calling to someone. A shot of Glenda answering was cut in. Then the camera followed Doreen back to the settee. She sat down. Albert was standing next to the settee feeling to see if the false moustache was going to hold. Doreen indicated the tea tray. Albert acted yes please and sat down next to Doreen. She poured the imaginary tea and handed it to him. For a minute or two they talked to one another, then Doreen accidentally tipped her invisible tea over Albert's trousers. Albert jumped up as if it was very hot. Doreen stayed sitting down and took a handkerchief from her sleeve and began to dab at Albert's trousers. The dabbing went on and on until it turned into a stroking motion. Albert stretched his hand out and put it at the back of Doreen's head and pulled her to him so that her head nestled against his trousers. He began to stroke her head. Doreen pressed her head hard against him. Eventually she reached up and unzipped his flies and put her hand inside. Albert unhooked the flat fastener and pushed his trousers down to a point just below his knees. Doreen pressed her face against his underpants and pushed her hand inside them via the leg. Gradually Albert sank down on to the settee and lay back. Doreen removed her hand from the leg of his pants and inserted both hands inside the elastic at the top and began to pull them down. The film cut to a different set-up, farther back from the settee, taking in more of the room. The door opened. Glenda appeared and stared in mock horror at what was going on on the settee. Albert pulled away from Doreen. Glenda dashed across the room. Doreen shrank away from her. Glenda pretended to slap Doreen's face. Then Glenda sat down on the settee and pulled Doreen across her and lifted Doreen's skirt and began to smack her arse.

I looked back at Glenda. She was breathing even slower than before and her eyes were shut. The whisky glass was on its side and a stain was spreading on the brilliant counterpane.

I shook her. Her eyelids flickered. I shook her again. She groaned.

'Glenda,' I said.

Words gurgled in her throat.

'Glenda.'

She opened her eyes. They swivelled about

in their sockets.

'You're on,' I said.

She closed her eyes and pressed herself deeper into the counterpane and stretched out her arms and legs like a cat on a mat.

I stood up and took hold of her wrists and pulled her clean off the bed and then let go. She hit the floor face first and screamed. One of her feet had caught in the counterpane and she'd dragged it off the bed and she began thrashing about on the floor, twisting the counterpane round her. The fall had caused her to split her top lip and when that got through to her she tried to put her hands to her face but by now the counterpane was tight round her and in her drunkenness she was making it tighter.

I grabbed the counterpane and yanked her up off the floor and punched her just beneath the ribs. She stopped screaming because she couldn't scream and try to breathe in at the same time. Her eyes were rolling madly and she was having trouble trying to work out what was going on. So I dragged her out of the bedroom and found the bathroom. I bundled her through the door and took hold of her at the back of her neck and pushed her face down into the bath water but as her arms were pinned to her sides she kept going forward and all of her went in. A wave of water splashed over the side and up the walls and into one of my shoes and over one of my trouser legs. I bent over the bath and pulled her up by her arms. The counterpane fell away and flooded the surface of the remaining bathwater. Glenda banged her kneecap on the edge of the bath as I pulled her out and she opened her mouth in pain but she didn't scream. Once her feet were on the floor I swung her back and sat her down on the edge of the bath, holding both her wrists together in one hand leaving my other hand free.

'Right,' I said. 'Now then. About the film.'

Her head lolled from side to side. Her eyes weren't fixing on anything. I slapped her face.

'The girl,' I said. 'Tell me about the girl.'

'The girl?'

'The girl in the film. Who pulled her?'

'I don't know.'

I slapped her again.

'Was it Albert?'

'I don't know. I don't know.'

'Do you know who she is?'

'No. She was new.'

'Who pulled her?'

'I don't know.'

'It's one of Kinnear's films, isn't it?'

She nodded.

'Who set it up? Eric?'

'Yes.'

'Then he pulled her. Didn't he?'

She didn't answer.

I took hold of her neck and twisted her round and pushed her head under again. I held it there for a while and she thrashed about and when I pulled her back up again she'd got the counterpane tangled round her head.

'Who pulled her?'

Her mouth opened and closed like the mouth of a dying fish. Water streamed from her nostrils and diluted the smudge of blood below her nose.

'Eric. It's usually Eric.'

'Why did they knock off Frank?'

'Frank?'

'Frank. My brother.'

'I don't know.'

'Did he find out?'

'I don't know what you're talking about.'

'You're a lying bitch.'

'I'm not. Honest.'

'What does Cliff know?'

'I don't know.'

'What was said after I left last night?'

'Nowt. I was lying.'

I raised my hand.

'Honest. I was lying. After you went, they stopped playing cards and then Eric went after you and came back and then them other fellers left and him and Cyril cleared off into Cyril's office. That's all that happened.'

I looked at her.

'Cliff's wasting his money, isn't he? You don't know fuck all.'

She opened her mouth to answer but I gave her a back hander and knocked her off the side of the bath. She lay in the pool of water on the floor, shivering.

I lowered the lid of the toilet and sat down and lit up.

'So you don't know who the girl was?'

She shook her head.

'Sure about that?'

'Eric called her Doreen. That's all I know.'

'And he didn't mention her second name?'

'No.'

'Shall I tell you what it is?'

She looked at me.

'It's Carter.'

I watched her face while that sank in.

'Her father was knocked off last Sunday.'

She began to slither slowly away from me but there wasn't very far she could go.

'My brother. Frank. As if you didn't know.'

She was up against the bath now, pressing herself against the simulated marble.

'And you don't know anything.'

She shook her head. She stopped doing that when she saw me take Con's knife out of my pocket.

'All I want you to tell me is two things,' I said. 'Who killed Frank. You know, the names, all of them. And why. But exactly.

238

What he'd actually done. And then I'll let your face stay as it is.'

She couldn't speak for a few minutes. I waited.

'God,' she said. 'Listen. I don't know. Believe me. When you came to "The Casino" last night, that was the first time I heard the name Carter, and that's the truth. I only knew that girl as Doreen. And I never heard anybody say anything about your brother. Christ, I'd tell you. I really would.'

'What about Cliff? What's he told you?'

'Nothing. All I know is what he told you. He doesn't tell me much.'

After a while I put the knife away. I stood up and threw my cigarette in the bath.

'Get up,' I said.

She didn't move. I opened the bathroom door and bent down and pulled her to her feet and pushed her through the door.

'Get in the bedroom,' I said.

She half fell into the bedroom and turned and stared at me. The square of light on the white wall was blank but still flickering. I walked past her and dragged open a dressing-table drawer.

'Get dressed,' I said.

'Dressed?'

'We're going out.'

'Where?'

'We're going to see if Albert knows any more than you do.'

'Why – why do you want me to come?'

'Don't be fucking stupid.'

She thought about it.

'Look,' she said. 'You can trust me. I won't tell. Just...'

'Shut up and get dressed before I make sure a different way.'

She began to get out of her wet under-wear.

'Besides,' I said. 'I'd like you to be there when I chat up Albert.'

She looked at me.

'Just in case, you know, you've not been telling me straight like.'

Now the late afternoon was solid grey. The wide dead expanse surrounding Albert's house was all one colour, a reflection of the uniform sky. Beyond the house the hot flashes from the steelworks were pastel behind the haze.

I bumped the TR4 across the soaked ground. Next to me Glenda was pressing the plaster she'd put on her lip to make sure it was sticking.

This time I drove straight round the back. The kitchen window was brilliant in the darkness of the back of the house.

As I pulled the handbrake on Albert appeared at the window. I opened the car door and Albert disappeared hooking his braces on to his shoulders. I yanked the keys from the dashboard and ran for the house. Glenda didn't have to be told what to do. She stayed where she was.

I opened the kitchen door but Albert wasn't there any more. Just Eddie Waring and Hull Kingston Rovers and St Helens and their supporters making a lot of noise in the corner.

I flung open the door Lucille'd come through the night before but there was just the old biddy making the bed. The room stank of carbolic. The old biddy froze and I slammed the door on her.

There was one other door and I opened it. There was a dark hall with oil-cloth wallpaper and at the end of the hall there was the front door which was open. I ran down the hall and out into the greyness. Albert wasn't anywhere in sight.

I ran along the front of the house and round the corner but he still wasn't there so I kept going and turned the other corner and I was at the back of the house again. Albert was there. Frozen in fright. He'd been running for the car but Glenda was screaming at him that I'd got the keys. Albert fucked and blinded and then Glenda screamed again having seen me and Albert turned and he saw me as well and then he began running away from the house and me in the general direction of the steelworks.

I walked over to the car. Glenda tried to

scramble out but I got to her before she could do that. I got in on the driver's side and pulled her down into her seat and gave her a couple of backhanders round her head. Then I inserted the ignition key in the dashboard and switched on and began to trundle the car after Albert.

When Albert heard the engine start, he looked over his shoulder and tried to run faster but the trouble was he couldn't. He was on his top wack already. It didn't take long for me to catch him up. I slowed the car down to his speed and let him carry on. Now his strides were getting longer and every time he looked over his shoulder to see what the distance was he stumbled and I could tell from the way he was running he was in agony with his breathing.

I stuck my head out of the window.

'What's up, Albert? Your tubes playing up are they?'

He staggered on.

'Keep going, Albert,' I shouted. 'Better not let me catch you.'

Albert was almost at the end of the waste ground. Here the ground sloped steeply away down to the outlying edge of the steelworks. I put my foot down and steered the car past Albert. He veered right and so did I. I drove alongside him, between him and the top of the slope.

'Any minute now, Albert? You've just

242

about had it.'

Albert pulled up sharp and before I could stop the car he ran behind it and started slithering down the slope. I swore and jammed everything on and snatched the ignition key from the dashboard. I got out and ran to the edge. Albert was about halfway down. At the bottom of the slope was a narrow gauge railway track curving back towards the steelworks. The track ran along the edge of another shorter slope, but Albert wouldn't be running down that one because that was where they tipped the molten waste and they'd just dumped a fresh load. Farther down the track an engine pulling some empty pans was receding into the greyness. Albert's best bet was to follow it back to the works where there were people about. When he got to the bottom that's what he did, but it wasn't any good because I charged down the slope on a diagonal track and I was ten feet behind him before he'd gone twenty yards.

He didn't stop running. He knew it wouldn't do him any good. But he kept going anyway. Until he fell that is. And even when he fell he kept going, trying to crawl to get back on his feet but it was no good because then I was on him, dragging him to his feet, pushing him against an up-turned pan by the side of the track, holding him by his windpipe, punching his face.

But I didn't do much punching. Not yet. I wanted him to tell me things first.

'Tell me all about it, Albert,' I said. 'Tell me about Doreen. Tell me about Frank.'

He couldn't speak. There wasn't enough breath in him. What there was rasped up and down his tubes like a cheese-grater. So I let go of his windpipe and I stood back and took out a fag and lit up. Albert bent double and braced himself by gripping his knees. He began to heave and pale bile began to fall from his mouth. Gradually the heaving and the bile got less and he relaxed the grip on his knees. He straightened up and fell back against the pan.

'For Christ's sake, give us a fag,' he said.

I gave him a fag. I even lit it for him. It seemed to make him better. He didn't even cough.

I let him have a couple of drags before I said:

'Now tell me, or I'll kill you here.'

'I know,' he said, taking another drag. 'I know.'

I waited.

'I didn't know who Doreen was,' he said. 'I didn't know that she was Frank's daughter. She was just another bird.'

'Eric pulled her didn't he?'

Albert massaged his brow with the heel of his hand.

'Yes, Eric pulled her.'

'How?'

'I dunno. He's got his ways.'

'When did you find out who she was?'

'About a fortnight ago.'

'How?'

He took another drag.

'Look,' he said. 'There's one thing. I had nowt to do with it.'

'With what, Albert?'

'With Frank. What happened to him.'

'Later, Albert,' I said. 'We'll come to that later.'

He sucked on the fag.

'Listen…'

'How did you find out who she was, Albert?'

He blew his smoke into the damp air.

'I had to. I had a visit from somebody.'

'Who?'

'Feller called Brumby.'

'Brumby?'

'Yeah. Said he'd seen the movie. Wanted to get hold of the young bird in it. For certain activities of his own, like. I said it couldn't be done. He said if it wasn't the Chief Constable'd be getting himself a nice lot of publicity closing down a certain brothel on the edge of town. So I found out. I mean, I couldn't go to Eric. Him and Kinnear would've dropped me like a brick if I'd been paid a visit.'

'How did you find out?'

'I found out, that's all that matters.'

'And you told Brumby?'

'That's right.'

'And shortly afterwards Frank got killed.'

He didn't answer.

'Why?'

He still didn't answer.

'Do you want to be dead, Albert?'

Another drag.

'See, it was Sunday afternoon. I was watching the football on T.V. and Eric comes in. With Frank and two boys of his. Only Frank's out. He tells me to clear Lucille and the kids off into the other room, but we have to go in the other room because if I shift the kids from in front of the telly...'

'Albert,' I said.

'Yeah, well, anyway. So Eric says Frank's rumbled. Somehow Frank's seen the movie. He's going to go to the button men. So I imagine they're going to duff him up in order to make him think twice, like. But Eric says no. Frank's not the type. Break his arms and legs and carve him up, do anything, but he'd still land us there. So I say what? Eric tells me. I tell him no, not here. He tells me not to be so fucking stupid. It's going to be an accident. Have I got any booze? I say yes, so he tells me to fetch a bottle and meantime the boys bring Frank round. When they've done that they hold him while Eric pours the stuff down his throat.'

'What did you do, Albert?'

'Nothing.'

I didn't say anything.

'What could I do?' he said. 'Tell me, what could I do. You know Eric.'

'Then what happened?'

'They'd got Frank's car outside. They took him away. That's all.'

'Did Eric know I was Frank's brother?'

'Yeah.'

'How?'

'I told him while he was pouring the stuff down Frank's throat.'

'Why?'

'To try and make him stop.'

'Oh yes?'

'Honest.'

'And what did Eric say?'

'He said Good, and went on pouring.'

I threw my cigarette away.

'Is that all there is?'

He nodded.

'Then that's it, Albert?'

Albert pressed himself hard against the pan.

'Jack for Christ's sake...'

'Don't be a cunt, Albert. You knew what I'd do.'

'Yeah, but listen. Christ, I didn't kill him. It wasn't me.'

I took Con's knife out of my pocket.

'I know it wasn't you.'

247

'Well, then...'

'Doesn't matter, Albert.'

I walked towards him. He fell on his knees and took hold of my trousers and began to cry. I remembered the film and I remembered how Doreen had been on her knees to him. I remembered the billiard hall like it was yesterday and I remembered Albert's dark eyes full of scorn for Frank as he'd lain there on the floor and I remembered my own disgust at Frank and my admiration for Albert. And I thought of how it must have been for Frank while they poured scotch down him and him knowing what they were going to do to him. I took hold of Albert's hair and pulled him to his feet by it and pressed him against the pan.

'Jack...'

I gave him the knife. I put it in just below the ribs, thrusting upwards. Albert's eyes and mouth opened wider than they'd done at any other time in his life. I left the knife where it was for a moment or two then I pulled it out very slowly, then put it back. Albert began to slide down the side of the pan in silence. I pulled the knife out for the last time and stood back and watched him die.

Then, when he was dead, I dragged him across the narrow track and along the edge of the slope to where they tipped the molten waste. It was still glowing orange from the last load. I let go of Albert's arms and bent down and rolled him over the edge but he didn't make the molten waste so I had to clamber down after him and lift him up and half throw him into the tip. The heat was so unbearable that I didn't have time to watch what happened to his body when it hit the surface. But I heard what the heat did with his vocal cords.

I didn't look back when I got to the top of the slope. I knew there wouldn't be anything left to see.

I climbed the other slope and walked back towards the car. Glenda wasn't there any more. I hadn't expected she would be. But she couldn't have got very far. Not far enough to get on the phone to Brumby. Although I was fairly sure she didn't know what Cliff was up to. Otherwise, she wouldn't have shown me the film, drunk as she'd been.

I got in the car and drove back to the house. Glenda wasn't anywhere around the house or between the house and the road. She must have run like hell.

But even so.

I stopped the car and went into the house. The kitchen was empty. Over in the corner the telly was churning out the football results. I looked through to where the old biddy had been. She wasn't there any more.

The bed was at the stage it had been at when I'd interrupted her.

I walked into the hall. Before me the front door was still open. I stopped and listened. Absolute silence. I started walking again and stopped when I reached the front door. I looked across the waste land to the road. Nothing. I turned away from the doorway and pulled the door to.

Behind the door was a straight backed dining chair and on the chair was a telephone.

I swore.

Then I hurried down the hall and across the kitchen and threw open the kitchen door.

Something moved.

It was the door to the outside toilet. A fraction. It could have been the wind.

I closed the kitchen door and walked towards the car and then when I was at my nearest point to the toilet, I rushed over and pulled the door wide open.

The old biddy was pressed in the corner against the pipes. Her mouth was opening and closing like a young sparrow at feeding time but she wasn't making any noise. She covered her head with her hands and shuffled her slippered feet about on the damp floor. I took hold of one of her arms and yanked her out.

'All right, Ma,' I said. 'Who's coming?'

She kept her head turned away from me. 'I said who's coming, Ma?'

She wouldn't answer. I pushed her away from me. I had to get after Glenda before she got to Brumby. I turned away from the old biddy to make for the TR4 but the sound of a car getting closer to the house stopped me. The car was moving fast. I was exactly halfway between the TR4 and the house. I decided which way I was going when a black Austin Cambridge rocked round the corner, making for the space between me and the TR4. I dashed for the kitchen door. The old biddy ran back into the toilet. We slammed the respective doors behind us.

The car stopped.

In the car, there was Eric, in civvies, Con, Peter, two boyos and a girl. The girl was Glenda. She was sitting on Con's knee in the front. They must have picked her up on her way down the road. Eric was behind the wheel. Nobody opened any doors.

I appeared at the window and looked at them all. Con said something to Eric and Eric nearly killed himself putting the car in reverse and manoeuvring it behind the back of the toilet.

I smiled. I'd nearly forgotten about Con's shooter. Nearly.

Not that I wanted to use it. The estate was too near. More than one shot and the streets'd be full of women in pinnies fetching bobbies and that would interfere with what I wanted to do.

So I took the shooter out of my pocket and raised the kitchen window and stuck my head out so I had a better view round the corner of the lav. They were all still sitting in the car. Eric was shouting at Con and Con was looking weary and the rest of them were sitting there like stuffed dummies.

I waved the shooter about and they all faced front.

'Here I am Eric,' I shouted. 'What's the matter?'

I took careful aim at Eric's face. Everybody did what I thought they'd do. Doors opened. Glenda was heaved off Con's knees on to the ground. Eric and the two boyos made for the back of the lav. Con and Peter stayed by the far side of the car, crouched down behind open doors. Peter tugged his big shooter out. Eric's voice crackled hysterically from behind the lav.

'No guns,' he screeched. 'Cyril said no guns, you stupid bastard.'

I bet he did, I thought. You can't sweeten crime squads by using shooters.

But the trouble was that at the same time as Eric was shouting, the lav door opened and the old biddy darted out. She'd no idea where she was going but she'd decided she wasn't staying in there any more. The lav door was between her and Peter so Peter couldn't see who it was but it didn't stop him letting go with two into the door.

'Kee-rist,' screeched Eric.

The old biddy swivelled round. The bullets had slammed the door to and she wrestled with the latch until finally she managed to get her fingers round it properly and then jerked the door open and closed it behind her.

'What are you trying to do? Get us all done?' Eric shouted.

'Get fucked,' said Peter.

He took aim at the window, resting his arm on the rolled down window of the door he was behind but Con who was in front of the door just reached up and took hold of the gun by the barrel and jerked it out of Peter's hand. Peter leant through the window of the open door and tried to get the gun back from Con.

'Give us the fucking gun back, Con,' he said. 'I've had enough of the bastard.'

'Leave it, Peter. Gerald'll want to see him first.'

I wondered why. The way he said it made it sound as if there was something I should know.

Peter gave over trying to get the gun and slid back through the window to his side of the door. He sat on the floor of the car and stretched his legs out in front of him and fucked and blinded to himself.

One of the boyos behind the lav said to Eric:

'I didn't know there was off to be any guns.'

Eric didn't answer.

'I mean,' said the boyo.

Eric told him to shut his bloody trap.

Then there was silence.

'Well,' I shouted, 'are you coming in? Or do we piss about all day?'

There was more silence. Then Eric's voice came from behind the lav full of rage and spite.

'You're finished, Jack. You know that, don't you? I've bloody finished you.'

'I'm not finished until I'm dead, Eric. And that won't be until after you are.'

Eric laughed.

'You're dead now Jack, only you don't know it.'

He laughed some more. If I hadn't wanted him the way I wanted him I'd have walked over to him and emptied the shooter into his face. That was the way his laugh made me feel.

'Tell him, Con. Tell him how I've fixed him. If he ever leaves here altogether that is.'

Con shifted a little before he spoke. Shifted back into the car so that I couldn't see any of him at all.

'See Jack,' he said, 'before we were summoned here, we were all having a little chat, me and Peter and Eric. Came up in conversation, like, the speculation around about you and Audrey. Eric thought it'd be only fair to Gerald if he was put in the picture. Give him a chance to talk to Audrey about it to see if it was true or not.'

Eric laughed again.

'Didn't believe us at first, did he, Con? Then Peter talked to him.'

'Didn't even say goodbye,' said Peter. 'Just asked us to take you back to him alive.'

'I should imagine Gerald'll be talking to her round about now, wouldn't you, Peter?' said Eric.

'Shouldn't be surprised.'

Christ. Audrey. He'd mark her. He'd do it good. It'd be the end of her. She'd kill herself afterwards.

My guts turned over.

I had to get to her. I hoped to God Gerald had been at his office when they'd phoned. That was the only chance.

I hurried across the kitchen and down the hall to where the phone was. I picked up the phone and sat down on the chair facing the kitchen door so that I could see if anything was going on. I put the phone and the shooter in my lap and picked up the receiver and dialled 'O'.

Eric's voice drifted in through the kitchen window.

'What do you think, Jack? Maybe you're kinky for birds with no faces.'

'Number please.'

'I want 01-333-8484.'

'01-333-8484. And what is your number please?'

'–5985.'

'Trying to connect you.'

The ringing tone began.

Outside there was silence.

The ringing tone carried on. She'd have answered by now if she'd been there. Been there on her own.

I flashed the operator. She was a long time coming back on the line.

'Look, can you get me 01-898-7436?'

'01-898-7436. Thank you.'

The ringing tone only went once before someone lifted the receiver.

'Maurice?'

'Yes, Jack.'

'Maurice, listen. You've got to get to Audrey. Gerald knows. You've got to get to her first.'

There was a slight pause before Maurice answered.

'How much time do I have?'

'Get on with it, Maurice. If Gerald gets to her first you're in the cart as well.'

Maurice hung up.

I sat there on the chair and stared at the hall but I didn't see anything. All I saw was what was in my mind: what I was going to do to them all. For everything.

Then the front door began to open.

Just a fraction at first. Then it stayed like that for a while. I sat very still. The door opened a bit more and stopped again. I stayed exactly as I was. The door swung open until it was about one hundred and twenty degrees to the doorway.

Then whoever it was stepped into the hall and waited.

It wasn't Eric because Eric's voice rang out from behind the lav.

'I wonder if you'll still fancy her when Gerald's finished with her, eh, Jack?'

Whoever it was stopped waiting and began to ease their way down the hall. Very slowly I moved my right foot until it was touching the door. Then I gave it a little push so that it slowly swung back away from me.

Peter froze in mid-tip-toe. I picked the phone up from my lap and put it down on the floor but I didn't get up. Peter hadn't moved.

'Put it on the floor,' I said.

He bent down and put his shooter on the floor.

'Stay there,' I said.

He stayed crouched down, squatting like a big frog, balancing himself with his finger-tips.

I stood up and walked over to him and

257

stuck the muzzle of the shooter against the back of his head.

'Now then,' I said.

Peter farted with fright.

'Don't,' he said, 'don't.'

He fell forward on his face. When he realised the shooter hadn't gone off he began to crawl along the floor towards the kitchen door. I strolled after him.

'What do you think Gerald'll do to Audrey, Peter?'

Words came out of Peter's mouth but they didn't mean anything. He didn't stop crawling. He crawled through into the kitchen and across the floor but he didn't try and get up because I was right behind him all the way. I stepped across him when he got to the back door and opened it for him so that he'd be able to crawl out and down the step.

Outside the scene had changed. Con was still behind the car door with Glenda, and Eric was still out of sight behind the lav but the two boyos were out in the open. One of them was pressing himself against the lav door staring at me and Peter and the other one was crawling along the ground by the wall of the house so that he couldn't be seen from the kitchen window. He didn't see me at first and carried on crawling towards the back door.

'Mick,' said the boyo against the lav.

258

The boyo on the floor looked up and saw Peter crawling over the kitchen step. The boyo stopped. But I wasn't interested in him or his mate.

'Come on,' I said to Peter. 'Tell me what Gerald's going to do to Audrey.'

Peter kept going. Now he was in the open, away from the back door.

'Peter,' I said.

Peter stopped crawling and lifted his head and looked round at me. I raised my arm and took careful aim at his left buttock. Peter's face crumbled.

I pulled the trigger. Various things happened.

First, the bullet tore flesh and twill away from Peter's arse. Then he screamed and tried to get his hands to the wound but he was twitching and writhing too much to be able to control himself. Second, both boyos detached themselves from their respective surfaces and took off like the wind down the side of the house in the direction of the road.

Eric dived for the car. I let one go at him but it hit the open door while Eric was behind it. He scrambled into the driver's seat and kept his head out of sight below the windscreen.

I looked beyond the car to the edge of the estate. A hundred yards away, a white patrol car was pulling up at the end of the one of the roads that ended on the edge of the waste ground. Doors opened and the button men got out and began to walk across towards the house.

Eric started the car. Con got in and Glenda tried to follow him but he pushed her away and slammed the door. Glenda threw herself back at the car but by then Eric, still out of sight, had begun reversing away at top speed. Glenda fell to the ground and screamed and cursed.

I looked down at Peter and stretched my arm out and pointed the shooter at his head. He stared up at me. His mind was almost gone with the pain but not enough not to know he was going to die.

I shot him through the forehead and walked over to the TR4.

By this time the button men had turned back and were racing for their car. Eric had got his car in top gear and pointed towards the road.

I got in the TR4 and swung it round the corner of the house.

In front of me, Glenda was stumbling after Eric's car. Beyond the car the two boyos were still running. They waved at Eric as the car overhauled them but he took no notice. He'd rather risk them talking to the button men. Eric wasn't stopping for anybody.

I caught up with Glenda and stopped and threw open the passenger door, just as she'd done earlier for me.

She bundled herself in. She hadn't much choice. As I took off I looked in the driving mirror. The patrol car was almost at the house. I put my foot down.

When I was almost at the road I looked in the mirror again. The patrol car had stopped in front of the boyos. One of the button men jumped out and waited for them to come to him. The patrol car started moving again.

I squealed the car on to the road and as I straightened up I noticed a group of people walking down the opposite side of the road towards the waste ground. There were two women and two kids and one of the women was pushing a pram. Lucille and Greer and the kids returning from the afternoon's shopping. Well, there'd be more than *Dr Who* to look forward to when they got home.

I was going hard but so was the patrol car. I overtook Eric and Con and we all exchanged impassive glances as I turned right at the top of the road. I expected the button men to stick with something they could catch but they turned right as well.

On my right was the estate. On my left were rows of old terraced houses leading back to the High Street. If I couldn't shake the patrol car I was in trouble. If I did shake it, I was still in trouble. There'd be an all cars alert out by now and a white TR4 wasn't going to get very far in this town. I had to get rid of it.

I turned left into one of the terraced streets. I accelerated up the road and turned sharp right just as the patrol car was coming round the corner. I gave it as much as I could and turned left before the patrol car was in sight again. Then left again and right.

I threw the brakes on. Glenda nearly went through the windscreen. I twisted round in my seat and gave her one that laid her out cold. Then I got out of the car and ran round to her side and dragged her out into the road and left her lying there. That'd keep the button men occupied for the little time I needed.

I ran across the road and down a passage. I crossed the back gardens and went down another passage and came out in the next street.

There was an alley at the top of the street. I knew it led to the back of United's ground. Which was where I wanted to be. I looked at my watch. The match was just finishing. If the button men didn't come screaming down the street I'd just make it. I'd make it even if they did.

I started to run.

The patrol car came round the corner when I was about two houses away from the entrance of the alley.

I ran even faster and turned the corner. I could hear the murmur of the crowd coming away from the match. The alley was L-shaped and a few supporters turned the corner in front of me, walking towards me. I ran past them and they looked but they didn't stop. The patrol car stopped at the end of the alley and the button men piled out. I turned the corner into the other half. More supporters. I could just make the end before the alley was flooded with them. Which would screw up the button men good and proper.

I squeezed past a bunch of supporters at the other end. Now I was in the open but I was among hundreds of chattering blokes. The button men didn't have a chance.

I pushed my way through the crowd towards the car park. Now there were even more supporters milling about. Damp macs stank in the rain. I came to the edge of the car park. The crowd was thinner here. I walked the paths between the cars looking for Brumby's Rover.

But before I saw the car I saw Brumby. He was talking to a pair of fat smoothies who looked very municipal. They were standing on the edge of the car park near one of the ground's exits guffawing at one another, all wanting to get away.

I looked back towards the crowd. Any minute now and a button man might be shoving his face through. There was no point in hanging about.

'Mr Brumby,' I called.

Brumby swivelled his head round and looked at me across the tops of cars. The others gawped too, but half at me and half at Brumby.

'Mr Brumby, could I have a word?'

There was nothing Brumby could do about it but to say his goodbyes and weave his way between the cars to where I was.

He didn't ask me what I wanted. He just stood there trying to make up his mind which expression he should be wearing.

'I want to talk to you,' I said.

He didn't ask me what about.

'Where's your car?'

'Over there.'

He pointed with his head without taking his eyes off me. I didn't have to tell him what to do. We walked down the avenue of cars to where his Rover was. He unlocked his door and got in and unlocked the passenger door. I glanced towards the crowd. Still no signs. I got in next to Brumby.

Brumby was sitting half turned towards me with an arm on the back of his seat. Just like at Glenda's.

'Well,' he said.

'We're going back to Glenda's.'

'What for?'

'I'll tell you when we get there.'

'Now look...'

'You look, Cliff. You look,' I said. 'Or don't you want Kinnear fixed?'

Brumby was silent for a minute or two.

'What made you change your mind?'

'Glenda's, Cliff.'

Cliff decided to take us to Glenda's. He faced front and began to ease the Rover out of the space and into the aisle. We joined the queue of leaving cars. I caught sight of the button men at the edge of the crowd. They were trying to push their way back towards the alley. They'd made a right muck-up. They should have stayed in their car and radio'd for help before chasing after me. Now they had to go all the way back and do it by which time it'd be too late. No wonder Kinnear was such a cocky bastard.

A few minutes later and we were swinging left on to the glossy road that led to the High Street. Hundreds of steamy cyclists wobbled and swished around us. The Rover slowed down about fifteen cars back from the traffic lights. I took out my fags and offered Brumby one. As I was lighting us up a patrol car screamed in from the High Street and flashed past us back towards the ground. The lights changed and Brumby slid the car forward. I rolled the window down a little bit and dropped the match out through the gap. We turned left into the High Street.

Neon shimmered in perspective. The grey

afternoon was turning slightly blue.

'Let's have it, Jack,' said Cliff. 'What's gone off since I talked to you?'

'I've told you. Wait till we get to Glenda's.'

'Why all the fucking mystery?'

'What's the matter, Cliff? You sound worried.'

'Why should I worry?'

'I dunno, Cliff. You tell me.'

'I just wondered why you changed your mind. That's all.'

I inhaled and said nothing. Brumby turned right and we were off the High Street. Abruptly there were more rows of terraced houses. Lots of blokes walking on their own, all in the same direction, away from the match.

Five minutes later and Brumby was easing the Rover into the kerb. I could see he was wondering where the TR4 was.

'Glenda must be out,' he said, trying to work out why.

I didn't say anything.

We got out and walked round to the lift. Brumby kept looking back as if he expected the TR4 to appear out of nowhere.

I pressed the button and the lift appeared. We got in. I whistled to myself and Brumby frowned at his feet.

We got out of the lift and walked along the balcony to Glenda's flat. Brumby took a key out of his trouser pocket and unlocked the

266

door. I motioned him to go in first. He wasn't very keen on the idea but he forgot that worry when he stepped through and heard the sound that was coming from the bedroom.

The projector was still chattering away to itself.

Things occurred to Brumby. He stopped in the hallway and stared at the half open bedroom door. I stepped into the hall and closed the front door behind me. Brumby jerked and turned to face me.

'What...' he said but I interrupted him by saying:

'Let's go into the bedroom.'

The white wall was still flickering emptily. Brumby stared at it as if he was seeing something very interesting.

'Sit down,' I said.

He sat down on the bed and looked at it and wondered what had happened to the beautiful orange counterpane.

'Where's Glenda?'

'Shut up,' I said.

There was a small round table next to the bed and on the table there was a red telephone.

I picked up the receiver and dialled the operator and gave her Maurice's number.

There was no answer. I asked the operator to get me Audrey's number. She did and there was no answer.

I put the receiver back and sat down on the bed and put my hands in my pockets and stretched my legs and looked at the toes of my shoes.

'You'll gather I've seen the film,' I said.

Brumby said nothing.

'I'm surprised Glenda lasted as long as she did. Shuttling between you and Kinnear, that is. Seeing as she's such a lush.'

'Where is she?'

'That's unimportant.'

'Why did she show you the film?'

'That doesn't matter either.'

Silence.

'Anyhow. The point is I've seen the film. Also I know more than I knew two hours ago. I've had second thoughts about the deal you wanted to make. I mean, I'm going to do them anyway, but I might as well make a few bob on it, eh Cliff?'

Brumby took his fags out.

'What did you find out?'

'What you already knew, Cliff. What you wouldn't tell me.'

He stuck his fag in his mouth.

'Can't understand it,' I said. 'I mean if you'd told me then I wouldn't have walked out like I did, would I?'

'No, but...'

'Still, I suppose you had your reasons. Tell you what though. One thing I don't understand. How did Frank get to see the

268

film? I mean somebody showed it to him. But who? Can't figure that out at all. You wouldn't know anything about that, would you, Cliff?'

Brumby shook his head.

'You're a lying bastard,' I said.

He twisted his head round slowly, in jerky stages, until he was looking at me.

I smiled at him.

'Come on, Cliff. Tell us all about it.'

'About what?'

'About how Frank got to see the film.'

'Jack, I don't know.'

'Knock it off, Cliff. I've talked to Albert.'

He didn't say anything. He didn't look all that well.

'You've no need to worry,' I said. 'I'm not after you. Just the blokes that did it. You offered me a deal. I'll accept it. But first you're going to tell me what you know. The truth. I want the whole picture.'

He took some more drags and nearly went cross-eyed trying to figure out whether he should or shouldn't tell me the truth.

He decided he should.

'As I said, it wasn't till after you'd gone last night,' he said.

'What, Cliff?'

'That I found out you were Frank's brother. I phoned the Fletchers. They told me.'

'What did they say?'

'Not much. But they knew all about Frank. You could tell.'

'How?'

'Just something one of them said.'

'What?'

'I can't remember exactly. But it was something like Kinnear's interests being their interests. Something like that.'

I flexed my toes.

'So what did they tell you to do?'

'How do you mean?'

'Don't be bloody silly. Gerald and Les tell people to do things. What did they tell you to do?'

Brumby looked at his fag.

'Not to create any stink about Kinnear setting me up for you. They told me to stay out of it.'

'They didn't ask you for any help?'

'No.'

'I wonder why?'

Brumby let that one go.

'So,' I said. 'You find out I'm Frank's brother. How do you feel about that? How does it affect you?'

Silence.

'Cliff?'

'Well, you're after the blokes that did for Frank.'

'And?'

'Maybe you think I was one of them.'

'Why?'

Brumby shifted on the bed so that he was facing me.

'I had to do it,' he said. 'But I didn't know who he was. I didn't know he was your brother.'

'What did you have to do, Cliff?'

'I told you earlier they were going to do for me. I had to find a way of doing for them first.'

I didn't say anything. He turned away and was facing the wall again.

'I went through everything Glenda'd told me. About all the various operations they're involved in. You know what they are. One in particular set me thinking. The films and the photos. The stuff they sell to the Fletchers.'

He paused in case I wanted to say anything but I didn't.

'So where there's that stuff, there's pulling. And it always goes better when there's young talent involved. The younger the better. No limit. But it's dicey. You only have to pull one wrong bird once. Even certain scuffers I'm acquainted with couldn't stop that one. That's why Eric's working up this way. He's very good. Very safe. They'd have to be very unlucky to cop it with Eric handling that side of the business.'

'So you made them unlucky,' I said.

He nodded.

'There was nothing certain about it. There

271

was only a chance it might work. But I had to try something. I asked Glenda if she'd been in anything with any young birds. She got hold of this one and I asked her if she knew the bird's name. But she didn't. So I went to see Albert. He told me who she was.'

'Did Glenda know what you were up to?'

'No, she never asks about things. She does as she's told and that's it.'

'So then what did you do, Cliff?'

'What?'

'When you found out who the girl was.'

'I did some checking up. Found out where she lived so I could find out what her folks were like. I had to know as much as I could about her folks because I was gambling on the kind of people they'd be. I mean, they could react two ways: they could beat the shit out of her and padlock her to the bed. They might even leave town. Most people'd keep something like that inside the family. On the other hand they might feel so outraged at what happened to their little girl that they'd want to nail the blokes that did it. Get the scuffers on to them. And the scuffers would have no choice. The papers'd be on to it like Jack Sharp. Things would have to be done. Topping jobs. Whoever it was.'

He stood up and went over to the dressing table and screwed his fag out.

'Only it didn't work out. I mean, I was right about your brother. About what he'd do. But he was stupid. He didn't go to the scuffers. He went to Eric instead.'

'How would he know Eric had owt to do with it?'

'Maybe he beat it out of Doreen.'

'Maybe,' I said.

There was a silence. Brumby stayed near the dressing table watching me. Half his face reflected the light from the projector.

'So what are you going to do?' he said.

I said nothing.

'I mean, it's Eric you want. Not me. I didn't know it was your brother. I didn't know it'd work out this way.'

I turned my head in Brumby's direction and smiled.

'Don't worry, Cliff,' I said. 'You offered me a deal. I want Eric and you want Kinnear. I told you. I only wanted to know the full story.'

Brumby looked at me.

'So where's the money?' I said.

'You'll do it?'

'I've told you, don't worry.'

He stood there for a few seconds and then very quickly walked out of the bedroom. I got up and followed him. He went into the kitchen and opened the fridge door. I stood in the doorway and watched him take the briefcase out of the fridge. Brumby straightened up and looked into my face.

'It was Glenda's idea,' he said.

I didn't say anything.

'About Glenda...' he said.

'I know as much as you,' I said. 'I came back and chatted her up to see if she'd tell me what you wouldn't. In the course of things she got randy and ran the movie. Then I thought I'd go and see Albert.'

'So you don't know where she is?'

I spread my hands.

'I know as much as you,' I said.

He looked down at the briefcase and frowned, then began to walk towards the door. I stood back to let him pass. He paused in the doorway.

'Jack...' he said.

'Don't worry, Cliff. You're all right.'

He walked past me and went into the lounge and sat down on the divan and placed the briefcase on the table the way he'd done earlier. I sat down opposite him, just to complete the pattern.

He opened the briefcase.

'Listen,' he said. 'With Kinnear out of the way, there'd be his machines. Maybe a few more bits and pieces. I couldn't take them, not on my own. But with you, on a partners basis...'

'Look, Cliff,' I said. 'Stop wasting your money on insurance. I don't want you. I've told you, just the deal as before.'

Brumby breathed in and took out the two bundles of very new notes and put them on the table. I didn't touch them. Brumby looked at me.

'And the rest,' I said.

Brumby carried on looking at me but his expression didn't change. Eventually he slid his hand into the briefcase and laid two more bundles of the same size on the table. I smiled at him.

'Never sell yourself short, Cliff,' I said. 'After all, it's your life. You've only the one.'

Gradually he relaxed and let himself give some sort of a smile.

'So,' he said.

'Where's Kinnear's place?'

'Near Sowerby. He's got an estate. It's off the Doncaster Road.'

'I know. You go through Malton.'

'When will you do it? Tonight?'

'Maybe.'

'Kinnear's got a party on. A weekend do. Supposed to look like a house party. Except it's not. Glenda's going. A few foreign clients. A few interesting diversions laid on. Down in the basement, like. He's got it all kitted out down there.'

'I can imagine.'

'Perhaps that's where Glenda is now,' he said, looking at me.

'Perhaps.'

He looked away.

'Well,' he said. 'We may as well have a drink on it.'

'May as well.'

Brumby poured the scotch. We drank.

'To Kinnear,' I said.

Brumby poured some more.

'What will you do?' he said. 'Let me know?'

'Maybe. It depends.'

'On what?'

'Things.'

We drank again. Brumby poured himself another. Very large.

'Not for me,' I said.

I stood up and Brumby finished his drink and stood up too.

'Anyway,' he said. 'I suppose I'll know soon enough.'

'I suppose you will.'

He clicked the briefcase shut and picked it up. I picked up the money and shoved it in my pockets. Brumby shrugged his overcoat closer round him and walked into the hall. The projector was still going full belt.

'Better shut it off,' I said.

I went into the bedroom. Before I switched the machine off I picked up the film and put it in its box and slipped it in my inside pocket.

Brumby was standing by the open door. I joined him and we went out into the grey day. Brumby closed the door behind us.

There was no one else about. We walked towards the lift. The misty rain was dense enough to practically obscure the neighbouring blocks. Only dull lights spreading soft at the edges were evidence of the other flats.

As we walked along the balcony Brumby was talking to me about how glad he was that everything had finally worked out all right, how he'd been a bit worried about telling me what he knew, etc, etc. The cold air and the warm scotch had made him a bit light-headed. He was like a man talking to himself.

We stopped outside the lift. I pressed the button. Somewhere down below a door slid to.

I turned round. Brumby was standing behind me leaning on his elbows against the parapet. He was still talking about something or other. He looked very expansive with his coat undone and his casual sweater gleaming in the blueness. I walked towards him. He stopped talking in mid-sentence. He didn't move. It was as though he'd turned to stone. Then his brain registered what I was going to do to him. His head jerked from side to side as he looked over his shoulder at the drop behind him. Then his head stopped jerking and he stared at me again and he knew that he wasn't going to be able to do a thing about it. I smiled at him and raised my arms to take hold of him.

Then the lift doors opened. There was a movement behind me and I automatically turned round and standing there staring at the pair of us was a woman in a headscarf carrying her Saturday afternoon shopping. The three of us stood there for a second, frozen in the blue afternoon light. But not for long. Brumby took off along the balcony towards the fire escape and the woman's jaw dropped and I whirled round and set off after Brumby but my foot slipped on the balcony's greasy surface and I went sprawling to the floor. I picked myself up but by now Brumby was on the fire escape taking the steps three at a time. The woman was still standing in the same position except her mouth was open a little bit wider. I began to rush along the balcony. Then I stopped. Something on the road beyond the green turf that surrounded the flats had caught my attention. Something white. Something with four wheels and moving very fast. Something with the word POLICE on it. Glenda had obviously not been backward in coming forward.

I looked over the parapet. Brumby was on the last flight of the fire escape, still haring down, oblivious of everything except his fear. He was going so fast that when he hit solid ground he almost came a cropper. But not quite. He carried on running, not

278

breaking his rhythm, taking a wide tack across the grass towards his Rover, his beautiful overcoat billowing out behind him. But the thing was that the police car was also making for the Rover, signifying interest by slowing down and then, as Brumby got closer to his car, the police car stopped abruptly, then started again at twice the speed and changed direction, mounting the kerb and driving across the grass towards Brumby, who had changed direction too, but it wasn't going to do him any good at all.

I turned and ran back to the lift. The woman was still standing there, her eyes watching me all the way into the lift. The only time I saw her move was as the door began to close and it dawned on her that some of her shopping was still in the lift.

The lift started down and I took out a fag and lit up and then the lift stopped and the door slid open and I walked away in the opposite direction to the one Cliff had chosen, underneath the flats, towards the garages where my car was, not looking back, not needing to, knowing that they had probably met by now, that he was commanding their full attention, making it nice for me.

Well, I thought, that was one way.

I walked round to the driver's side of the car and got in. I drove off and looked in my

279

driving mirror. I took the first turning on my left and picked up speed but not too much. I didn't have time to change cars.

I drove to a small post office I knew on the edge of town. It was closed but the lights were still on and I knew that all I'd have to do was to tap on the door.

I parked the car and walked across the road. In the window there were Christmas annuals and Dinky toys and games in big glossy boxes. Inside a woman of about fifty was sitting behind the grille on the post office side of the shop entering figures into an old fashioned ledger.

I tapped on the glass panel in the door. The woman looked up. I tapped again. Her lips moved. A man about the same age appeared from the back of the shop. He wore glasses and a brown cardigan. He walked over to the door. He didn't look very happy.

'I'm sorry,' I mouthed through the glass. 'I have to have some stamps. And an envelope.'

The man weighed me up. He looked at the woman. The woman was chewing the end of her biro. Eventually the man put the door on a chain and opened up.

'How many stamps?'

'About five bob's worth.'

'What sort of envelope?'

'A stiff backed one. About ten inches long.'

The man went away and got an envelope. The woman tore the stamps out of the book and the man picked them up on the way back.

'That'll be five and ten,' he said.

I got my change out and counted out the right money and handed it through the gap. The man passed me the envelope and the stamps.

'Thanks very much,' I said.

'Sorry about the caution,' the man said. 'Can't be too careful these days.'

'You're right,' I said. 'You never know.'

I walked away from the door. I took out my Biro and wrote a name and an address on the envelope and stuck the stamps down. Then I took the film out of my pocket and put it in the envelope and sealed it. I didn't drop the envelope into the post box because I had to make a phone call first. There was a box on a grassy island in the middle of the road.

Inside the box I put the envelope on top of the phone book and lifted the receiver and asked the operator to get me Maurice's number.

This time he was there.

'Maurice?'

'Yes.'

'What's happened?'

'The worst.'

'Tell me.'

'Gerald. He got to Audrey.'

'Where is she?'

'Here.'

'How's that?'

'Gerald did her at the house. Then he called Camm to fix her up there so she wouldn't have to go in hospital.'

'And?'

'Gerald left Camm there on his own. Tommy and I got her out after Camm had treated her.'

'What's she like?'

'A write-off.'

So that was that. Now there was Gerald as well as the others. Eventually Maurice said:

'Jack?'

'Yeah, listen. You get her out of it, right? Tomorrow, Monday, whenever she can be moved. Same plan. But get her away.'

'Right. What shall I tell her about you?'

'Nothing.'

'She'll want to know. She might not go if I don't tell her something.'

'All right. Tell her I'll follow her next week. Tell her it's taking longer than I thought. But make it sound good. Make her believe it's the truth. Otherwise she won't go and that won't do.'

'Maybe you should talk to her. Later tonight.'

'No,' I said. 'No, I don't want to do that.'

Maurice didn't say anything.

'And make sure she's got enough money.'

'Yes, Jack.'

Another silence.

'Also,' I said. 'Where can I get some white stuff?'

'White stuff?'

'Yes. Round here.'

'Nowhere. Not where you are. Unless you drove to Grimsby.'

'Who would I see?'

'Man called Storey. You'd find him upstairs at a coffee bar that calls itself a club. "The Matador", would you believe.'

'Will he do as he's told?'

'Yes.'

'Phone him and tell him I'm coming to see him.'

'When?'

'Sometime tonight. During hours.'

'Right.'

'I'll be seeing you.'

'When?'

'I'll let you know.'

I put the phone down and walked back across the road to the post box and pushed the envelope in the slit.

Now the darkness was complete. Wilton Estate retreated behind the rain. I drove down the road where I'd dropped Doreen and slowed down as I approached the corner of the crescent where Doreen was staying. I picked up speed again as I crossed the mouth. There was a patrol car parked half the way up on the right, outside the house Doreen had gone into earlier.

I swore and kept on going. I turned left into the road running parallel to the crescent and stopped the car. Rain pattered on the roof. I lit up and thought. I had to see Doreen because there was something she had to tell me if what I'd planned was going to work. Apart from the other reasons I had for seeing her.

I got out of the car. Leaving it there wasn't good. The scuffers'd be with Brumby by now. The scuffers with Doreen probably wouldn't have the number yet but it'd be waiting for them once they got back into their cosy little motor.

I walked across more wet grass and picked my way through more back gardens until I thought I was within a garden or two of where Doreen was staying.

A back door opened. Light streaked through the rain. I ducked down behind a sodden privet. Two scuffers were silhouetted against the glaring kitchen. A man and a woman gazed earnestly into the scuffers' faces. Between the two couples stood Doreen. In the light from the kitchen she looked pale and stark. Words were said and the scuffers stood back to let Doreen pass and then they waddled off after her in that way they all have. The back door was closed very respectfully. A few seconds later the doors of the patrol car opened and closed and the engine was turned on but the bastards didn't move. They were probably sitting there enjoying listening to my licence number. It must have been getting on for five minutes before they took off. I listened to them go. They were moving back towards the High Street. Away from where my car was parked.

I swore again. This time at Glenda. And at myself for leaving her to the scuffers.

I went back the way I'd come. The car was still there. There were no scuffers making little notes in little books. I got into the car and drove off down the estate, away from the High Street. I was back amongst the terraces.

It didn't take long to find the kind of motor I wanted. It was a little Morris Traveller, parked on some waste land at the end of the street. Tucked under some corrugated sheeting stemming from the wall of a builders yard. I parked next to it and got out. It didn't take long. A bit of jiggling with the fuses and it was away. The window was easy. Just like the old days. I transferred the shotgun and the shells and my hold-all into the back of the Traveller and that was that.

This time I didn't bother to knock up Keith's landlord. The front door was unlocked so I went straight up.

He was lying on his bed smoking. A transistor was balanced on his chest. Radio One was faint and tinny. On the bed there were *Reveilles* and *Tit-Bits* and a well-read *Daily Mirror.*

Only Keith's eyes moved when he saw me. The rest of him was still too stiff.

'Keith, where does Margaret live?'

'Get stuffed,' he said.

'Yeah, all right. Where does she live?'

Keith made a very big job of blowing smoke straight up towards the ceiling.

I sat down on the edge of the bed and took hold of him by his collar and jerked him towards me. The transistor slid off his chest and on to the floor.

'Listen,' I said, 'this is me you're talking to. Tell me, where does she live?'

'Why should I tell you fuck all?'

'Because you were a mate of Frank's.'

He looked at me.

'What do you know?' he said.

'I haven't time. You'll read all about it. Just where she lives that's all.'

He carried on looking at me.

'Don't worry,' I said. 'I only want to talk to her.'

'Sure.'

'Through her I get the ones that did for

Frank. That should matter to you.'

He looked away from me. After a while he said:

'She lives in Farrier Street.'

'Frank told you that?'

'Frank told me that.'

I let go of him.

'Who did it?' he said.

I stood up.

'I've told you. Just keep reading the papers.'

The woman in the off-licence on the corner of Farrier Street enjoyed giving me the number of Margaret's house. I'd hardly closed the door behind me before the woman had disappeared from behind the counter into the back of the shop to spread the glad tidings about Margaret's new feller. At least Margaret'd told the truth on one count.

I drove slowly down the street until I got to 19. I parked a few houses beyond and got out and walked round the back of Margaret's house. The kitchen was dark but there was a light in the dining-room. The sound of a telly gurgled beyond the curtains.

I opened the back door and walked through the kitchen and into the hall and opened the door to the dining-room.

Full ashtrays decorated the top of the

mantelpiece. The dining table was the way it had been at breakfast time. The hearth hadn't been swept for a week.

Margaret was lying on the sofa watching Rolf Harris and smoking. She was wearing a quilted housecoat patterned with pink roses. The housecoat wasn't fastened. Underneath it she was wearing an old black bra and a pair of old white nylon briefs. No stockings. Still wearing her dark glasses. She certainly wasn't expecting any boy-friends.

When she saw me and the look on my face she screamed and tried to crawl into the corner of the settee.

I switched the telly off and walked towards her. She stopped moving. I sat down on the arm of the settee and stretched my arm towards her face. She wanted to scream again but she couldn't. I took her dark glasses off. Her eyes were screwed up tight.

I dropped the glasses on the cushions.

'Was it easy?' I said.

She didn't answer. Her eyes were still tight shut. They snapped open when I began to run my fingers through her hair.

'How did you manage it?' I said.

She shuddered. I gripped her hair and jerked her head back. The cigarette fell from her hand on to the settee. I picked it up and held it an inch from her throat.

'How did Frank know who to go to? How did he know it was Eric?'

She squeezed her eyes shut again. Then she screamed as the tip of the cigarette got closer to her neck. Words gabbled out of her.

'I'll tell you. I'll tell you.'

I let go of her hair and sat and waited.

'Frank came round here. Sunday morning. A mate of his had got hold of the film. He'd guessed I'd had something to do with it. Only the thing was, Eric was here. Trying to get me to fix Doreen up for another session.'

'And what happened?'

'Eric wasn't on his own. They took Frank away.'

She bent double and took hold of her hair and pulled at it as if she was going to tear it out.

'Oh, bloody Christ,' she said. 'Bloody, sodding Christ. I didn't want to do it. I didn't. Not to Frank. Only it was Eric. He forced me. He made me.'

'You worked for him in the smoke?'

'A couple of times. Only once something went wrong. They went too far with a little coloured kid. And ... and...'

She began to sob. I pulled her upright.

'You lying whore. Stop giving me that shit. He paid you, didn't he? That's why you did it. Because he paid you.'

'No, honest, I...'

I brushed the cigarette against her cheek. She screamed much louder than before so I threw the cigarette on the floor and jammed my hand in her mouth. She tried to bite it, so I pulled it out and gave her one across the face. She fell sideways across the settee and started sobbing again.

I stood up.

'Get up,' I said.

She stopped the sobbing and looked up at me.

'We're going upstairs,' I said. 'Then we're going out.'

'Upstairs?'

'That's right.'

'But…'

I took out my fags and lit one up and held it in a certain way.

She got up off the settee and began to walk past me out of the room, trying to keep her eyes on me as she went.

I followed her upstairs. She kept looking back at me trying to see what was behind my eyes. On the landing I said:

'Let's go into your room.'

She opened a door. I took hold of her wrists and pulled her into the bedroom. She was too frightened to pull away.

Besides the bed, there were only two other pieces of furniture in the room. One of them was a big brown wardrobe. The door was open. Clothes that weren't on hangers had been thrown over the top of the door. Still holding on to her wrist I found a dress that looked newer and cleaner than any of the others. It was black with big white polka dots and a white lace ruffled collar. I threw it on the bed and then we went over to the remaining piece of furniture which was a white-wood dressing table. I opened the drawer until I found a black lace bra with matching pants and a black silk half-slip, the kind of stuff you see advertised in *Penthouse*.

I let go of Margaret's wrist and pushed the underwear at her.

'Put these on.'

Her eyes were wide.

'Do you want me to do it for you?'

She still didn't move.

I pushed the housecoat off her shoulders.

'Listen whore,' I said. 'You're going out. Dressed or undressed. Make up your bloody mind.'

She began to get dressed.

Rain sped past the black windows. The windscreen wipers groaned and whirred. Wind buffetted the car in flurries of whining irritation.

Dark trees flashed by.

I knew the road well. But I'd known it better in the summer. In biking weather. When Frank and I had done the same journey in a morning. Just to spend the whole afternoon on the ochre mud they call a beach. In spitting distance of the gasworks and smelling distance of the fish docks. But it was the journey there that'd made it good. The expectation, the excitement, the dry road crackling under our tyres, the warm wind flicking the collars of our open-neck shirts. The elation when we spotted an M.G. or an Alvis or the time when we'd actually found a Lagonda, hood down, parked on the grass verge, empty. We'd stopped and still straddling our bikes we'd carefully scanned the surrounding woods for any signs for someone who might have been associated with the car. But there'd been no one. So we'd dropped our bikes on the grass and sauntered over and looked around some more before actually touching it. I remembered the marvellous feeling of the mudguard warm from the sun under my palm. Frank hadn't touched the car at all. He'd just walked round it keeping a couple of feet between him and the car at all times. And then when still nobody had shown up I'd suggested to Frank that we got in, just to feel what it was like to sit in it. Of course Frank wouldn't. So I'd climbed in and sat in the hot leather seat behind the wheel and ran my hands over the walnut dashboard and I'd felt the thrill of fear as I noticed that the keys had been hanging from the dashboard. I'd just been stretching out my hand towards the ignition when Frank had yelled there'd been somebody coming and

I'd jumped out like a scalded cat and we'd leaped on our bikes and pedalled like bloody hell for a couple of miles.

Of course there hadn't been anybody coming at all. Frank had just put the wind up me to get me out of it. I'd had to laugh, afterwards.

There was a movement behind me. A shoe scraped against one of the rear doors. Nothing happened for a minute. Then there was more movement. The movement became frantic. Lips fought against sticking plaster. Wrists ground against rope and against each other. The movement reached its climax and then there was an exhausted silence.

Trees and hedges began to disappear. The road began to broaden out. Houses sped by more frequently. Sodium street lights regularly illuminated the rain.

I lit a cigarette and rolled down the window and threw the match out. Wind roared in my ears. It felt fresh and good. I left it rolled down and breathed in. Even now I could smell the fish dock.

Storey had very long hair, parted in the middle. He wore a flowered shirt with a high collar, a kipper tie patterned with fleur de lys, a grey herring-bone suit and black boots. Circular glasses with gold frames decorated the end of his nose. I would have said he was about twenty-five at the most.

His room was done out like an A and R man's office.

On one wall there was an original poster for *King Kong*. On another there was Humphrey Bogart. There was a fruit machine behind his desk that had been painted in pop colours. I wondered if it was one of Cliff's.

Music thumped from the juke-box downstairs.

Storey looked at me from behind his desk.

'So you know Maurice, do you?' he said.

'I'm surprised you do,' I said.

He smiled.

'The scene has changed,' he said. 'The scene has changed.'

I didn't say anything. Neither did he.

'Well?' I said.

'Well what?'

'Have you got it?'

'Oh, man. Come on. I mean, how much do you want, what quality, when? You don't think I keep it here?'

'I don't know where the fucking hell you keep it. Maurice told you what I wanted.'

'No, man. All he said was you'd be over to see me. That's all. What do you think this is, a supermarket?'

'I haven't much time.'

'So tell me what you want.'

The record on the juke-box stopped.

Voices growled below.

'I want a syringe. Made up. Two grains at the most.'

'Oh, man.'

'You'll get more than it's worth. Provided we don't have to chase all over the place.'

'But Maurice said…'

'Forget what Maurice said. Have you got it? Here?'

'Oh, come on. Why would I?'

I took some notes out of my wallet and put them on his desk.

He looked at the notes.

'I want a syringe,' I said. 'Made up. Two grains at the most.'

I walked along the cobbled street to where I'd left the car. There was the misty smoky taste of the river in the air. The rain had eased of and the wind wasn't so strong and the sounds of the docks swished and clanked across the night.

I got in the car and stretched over the back of my seat and lifted Margaret's coat away from her face. She stared up at me from the floor. I dropped the coat back over her face and she began to thrash about again,

I started the car and made a U-turn and began to drive away from the docks.

My headlights stroked the road-sign. Malton, it said. I knew it very well. Or used to. A village three miles away from Sowerby. Even smaller than Sowerby. Fifty inhabitants at the most, even these days. Only a few lighted windows gave away its existence. I slowed down. There were no street lights. The road curved and rose as it left the few houses behind. I coasted round the bend and there was a phone box shining like a beacon on the grass verge. I rolled the car level and got out. Wind raced through the grass and rushed through the branches of the great trees that lined the road.

In the phone box I opened the directory and found the name I wanted. I put the four pennies in the box and dialled the number.

I had to wait a long time. Then a man's voice said:

'Mr Kinnear's residence?'

'Ah,' I said. 'Could I speak to Mr Kinnear please?'

'I'm afraid he's busy at present. He's not to be disturbed.'

'Tell him it's London. That'll disturb him.'

'I beg your pardon?'

'Tell him it's Gerald and he's in a hurry.'

'Well why didn't you bloody well say so?'

I heard the phone clatter as he put it down. Seconds later a door opened and the far off sounds of the party came over the line like the noise of the sea in a sea-shell. A few minutes later the sound was cut off and then somebody else lifted the phone.

'Gerald?' said Kinnear.

'No,' I said. 'It's Jack.'

The tone changed. He went into his routine.

'Well, Jack,' he said. 'I hardly expected to be hearing from you.'

'Thought they'd have picked me up by now?'

He gave me the laugh.

'Something like that. You've been a bad lad.'

'I haven't finished yet.'

More laughter.

'You don't stand a chance, mate. Even if you go back to the smoke you're dead.'

'Maybe.' I lit a cigarette. 'I suppose you know they've picked up Glenda.'

'I know that.'

'And Frank's daughter.'

'Yes, Jack.'

'Glenda didn't only work for you, Cyril. Brumby paid her to listen to what you had to say.'

There was a small silence.

'Now that,' he said, 'was something I didn't know.'

'He was the one who got the film to Frank.'

'I wondered about that.'

'He was trying to nail you, Cyril. And he nearly succeeded.'

'Well,' he said. 'The things you hear. You

wouldn't credit some of them. Would you, Jack?'

'You wouldn't.'

'Funny,' he said. 'I even heard that Cliff had been picked up by the button men.'

'Funnier still when you think of Cliff and Glenda down there at the button shop together, making themselves comfy.'

'I see your point, Jack,' he said. 'But I don't quite understand your solicitudes.'

'Well, Cyril,' I said, 'when Doreen finds out why her dad was knocked over it'll be like the Luton Girls Choir down there. And they're not all friends of yours. Those that aren't'll enjoy lending their amplifiers to the young ladies.'

'True,' he said.

'So soon there'll be Eric adding his voice to the chorus, won't there?'

'Perhaps,' he said. 'But after all, I can't be held responsible for the actions of my employees, can I? I mean, I know nothing of Eric's activities outside of his working hours, do I?'

'I thought it'd be something like that,' I said. 'Even better, though, if Eric was to go on his holidays. Off the scene, like. Then you could even weep on their shoulders, couldn't you?'

'I must say the idea had occurred to me, Jack. He's not exactly on display at the moment.'

'And besides, he's such a cunt.'

'I'm afraid I'm inclined to agree.'

There was a silence.

'Poor old Eric,' he said eventually. 'He was really sick when he found out he'd pulled your niece. Really sick.'

'Where would he start from?' I said. 'If he was going away?'

'Do you know Mawby?'

'I know it.'

'How well?'

'Very well.'

'Know the brickpits? Near Mawby Ness?'

'I know them.'

'Then you'll know the brickyard house. Right on the river?'

'Yes.'

'Bloke that looks after the beacons lives there. Friend of ours. I think I'd send Eric down there for a start.'

'And I suppose you'd tell him to hang about until somebody came for him. Somebody in a Morris Traveller, say.'

'Something like that.'

'About what time?'

'Between four and five in the morning. That'd be feasible. If you were talking in terms of tomorrow, like.'

Another silence.

'Of course,' he said, 'there's one thing.'

'Yes?'

'You go home afterwards.'

'This is home.'

'I mean the smoke.'

'Yes.'

Static burst on to the line for a second or two.

'You surprise me,' he said.

'I want Eric,' I said.

'Enough to leave me be?'

'No,' I said. 'It's just that I haven't time for the two of you.'

Kinnear laughed his laugh and put the phone down.

I went out of the phone box. A car took the corner too fast and straightened up and screamed off up the slight hill.

I got back in the car. There was no movement in the back seat. I started the car and drove slowly away. There was no reason for me to hurry. I'd got all night.

A few miles farther down the road and I was driving even more slowly. I didn't want to miss the entrance to Sowerby aerodrome. When I found it I switched off the head lights and bumped the car over the verge and rolled along the main runway until I came to a group of old black nissen huts. I drove the car behind them out of sight of the road and switched off the engine. Then I switched the car light on, got out of the car and walked round to the passenger side. I opened the door and pulled the passenger seat forward. I took the syringe out of my pocket and unwrapped it and placed it on the back seat. Then I leant into the back and turned Margaret over so that she was lying on her face. She thrashed about a bit but she soon gave up because there wasn't very much she could do about anything.

I picked up the syringe. It wasn't as difficult as I thought it would be. Her arms being tied behind her back made it just a matter of being careful.

She thrashed about some more before she went under, straight after she felt the point of the needle, but not for long. She was out in under three minutes. I hauled her over on to her back again. Her breathing was very slow and there was a line of sweat on her forehead. I lifted one of her eyelids. The pupil was a pinprick.

Then I climbed over her on to the back seat and put my feet up. I covered my legs with Margaret's coat and pulled my own coat more tightly round me and eventually dropped off to sleep.

I dreamt that I was lying on a beach with Audrey and she was wearing a bikini and she had a handkerchief over her face to keep the sun off. But it was very cold and the wind kept rippling the edge of the handkerchief and I was panic stricken in case the wind blew the handkerchief away from her

301

face. But I couldn't let her know how I felt so I had to lie there propped up on my elbow looking at her saying the kinds of things to her that she used to like me to say. Finally I couldn't take it any longer and I got up from her side and ran towards the sea and kept running until the sea was over my head.

Sunday

I woke up at quarter to three. Stiff as a bloody board. I unscrewed my hip flask and took a long pull then I dragged myself back into the driver's seat and made a U-turn back on to the runway.

When I got back to the road I turned right. Towards Sowerby. Five minutes later I was in the village.

I didn't have to look hard to find Kinnear's place. It was an old Georgian farmhouse. Three or four acres of land. Plenty of trees. Set way back from the road. The party was still in full swing and every light in the house seemed to be on.

I drove past the gates and carried on down the road for a hundred yards or so before I stopped the car. You never could tell. There might be his own personalized little squad car tucked out of sight up the drive to keep the gatecrashers out and the drunks in.

I waited for a while before I moved. Nothing happened. So I got out and walked to where the high boundary wall ended and stuck my head round the corner to see what we'd got.

We'd got some more wall.

I swore. I'd have to take her in through the main entrance. I looked back down the road to the gates. The road inclined downwards very slightly.

I walked back to the car and let the hand brake off. Then I closed the door and stuck my shoulder through the window and took hold of the steering wheel with my left hand and began to push.

I stopped the car a few feet away from the gates and then walked over to the driveway and stood there and listened. There were no sounds of car doors slamming outside the house. There was no sound of anything approaching up the road.

So I walked back to the car and got Margaret.

I drove back to the phone box at Malton. I was a long time getting an operator. When she came on the line I asked for a London number. She asked me to insert two and six. I put in the change I'd taken from Margaret's purse earlier on.

The phone rattled at the other end. The voice that answered was full of sleep.

'Scully. Yes?'

'It's Jack Carter,' I said.

After that had sunk in the voice was a little less rumpled.

'Yes?'

'I've got a story for you.'

'Go on.'

'Involves blue films, a killing, bent cops, drugs and a friend of a couple of people you've been trying to wrap the fish and chips in for a long time now.'

There was a long pause.

'It sounds beautiful,' he said. 'But I'm forced to wonder why it's coming from you?'

'The man who was killed was called Carter.'

Another pause.

'Does it have to be over the phone?'

'There isn't time for any other way.'

'All right. Go ahead.'

'There's a condition.'

'I thought there might be.'

'You handle the story the way I tell you to.'

'I can't guarantee that.'

'Yes you can. When you hear the story.'

'Go on.'

'Not far from where I am there's a party going on. Wild. Cardboard dungeons and things. Right now one of the guests is lying in the grounds full of heroin. She used to be my brother's girl-friend. Until he was killed. After he found out that this woman had pulled his daughter into a blue movie. The man who had my brother killed has enough influence with the local scuffers to make them decide it was accidental. At the same time the scuffers are having to talk to the two birds involved in the movie. One of them being my brother's daughter. The other works for the man I'm talking about. The chances are they'll try and keep things nice and private.'

'So what happens?'

'You get one of your local men to phone the scuffers about the bird in the grounds. He tells them he's been tipped off. The scuffers phone the man we're talking about and put him wise and then scream over themselves. But the trick is some of your boys are already there. With cameras and everything. Maybe even yourself if you leave the tip-off late enough. So then of course the scuffers have no choice but to put the pressure on the man we're talking about. And everything's all over the front pages.'

'It's beautiful,' Scully said.

'Especially as I've mailed you a print of the film in question,' I said. 'It'll be at your office on Monday morning. I should go through your mail yourself just this once.'

The track was only wide enough for one car at a time. There were the occasional stretches where at one time or another they'd got some old bricks and stuck them next to each other to make a surface but the rest of the track was stony and covered with fine red brick dust. On either side of the track were reeds and beyond the reeds the flooded brickpits stretched broadly under the faintly lightening sky. There was no wind at all and the rain had stopped.

The house was at the end of the track. Beyond the house was the raised bank of the river and on the left four crumbling kilns shaped like Aztec architecture rose above the roofless buildings of the brickyards. Nothing had changed since I had been there last. Twenty-three years ago.

A light was burning in one of the downstairs rooms of the house, its glare deepening the surrounding blue of the dawn. A figure appeared at the window and stared down the track at the approaching noise. I drew closer and the figure disappeared. I reached the end of the track and stopped the car outside the house. I switched the engine off. I could hear the dim sound of the river rushing by beyond the bank. The light went out and the front door opened. Eric appeared, carrying a hold-all. He closed the door behind him and began to walk over to the car.

I rolled the window down. He looked me straight in the face but I was still only a pale blur in the dawn light.

He was only six feet away from the car when he saw who had come to collect him.

He gave a short high scream and dropped the hold-all. Then he began to run.

I got out of the car and leaned back in and picked up the shotgun off the back seat. I propped it up against the car while I took the bottle of scotch from my bag. I put the bottle in my coat pocket and began to walk off after Eric. I had plenty of time and there was nowhere for him to go.

He'd run up the side of the bank and was making for the brick-works, stumbling along the cycle track that the brickyarders had worn into the bank in the old days. I walked up the side of the bank and followed him watching him disappear into the overgrown brickyard and when I couldn't see him any more I could hear him scrambling over miniature screes of bricks that had fallen from the decaying walls. The sound had the rattle of death.

Now it was getting lighter by the second and on my right the river was changing from purple to grey and I could see the opposite bank a mile and a half away. The tide was out and the mud rippled with dawn colours and from out in the middle of the river the sound of the lightship bell travelled quickly over the

307

vast flatness of the river and its banks.

I paused at the spot where the bank ran into the brickyard. The sound of Eric's running had stopped. I walked forward.

The yard was square. On my right the boundary was a long low kiln so old that its top was totally covered with grass. To the left and in front of me two low broken down walls occasionally protruded above the briar and the elderberry. On the left, facing on to the river, were the roofless shells of the tileries, half their original height due to natural decay and the erosion of the local kids. Beyond the tileries, out of sight, were the remains of the landing stage. In the centre of all this were the four main kilns, still solid, and two large vats, full of old bricks and rain water. Frank and me, we used to sit on the edge of the vats and throw bangers in and watch them fizz across the surface of the water.

I stopped again and listened. There was still no sound. I walked over to the tileries and looked in each one. He wasn't there. I didn't go beyond them. If he'd gone that far he'd still have been running when I'd come into the yard.

I looked in both vats. Nothing. So I laid the shotgun down on the edge of one of the vats and took out the bottle of scotch and put it next to the shotgun and began to climb up the face of the nearest kiln. The kilns were stepped at intervals of four feet and as lads the trick was to pull yourself up from step to step until you got to the top. But now I was twice the size and there was no problem.

When I got to the top I swivelled round on my backside and dangled my feet over the edge and looked down at the vat twenty feet below. I wondered if the shotgun would tempt him out. I doubted it. Not old Eric. I smiled to myself. When we'd been kids and Frank and I and some others had used to come here we used to play exactly this kind of game. We'd pick one of us to go off and get lost and we'd give him a quarter of an hour and then we'd all fan out and start tracking him. When you were caught you had to pretend you'd been shot by the person who'd found you. It was a great game, whether you were hunter or hunted. But it was only good when you were a hunter if the hunted was good at hiding. Otherwise it got boring because it was all over too quickly. So if the bloke that was being hunted was no good I'd let the others hare off after him and I'd stay behind and climb up the kiln and lie low and wait and I'd always spot the bloke some- where or other, thinking he was safe as houses. Then I'd stand up and shout bang and he'd almost kill himself trying to see where my voice had come from.

But of course if it was Frank I never

bothered. It was one of the few games he ever took seriously. I'd always know where to find him, but I never did. I'd leave it to one of the others. But on the other hand I'd never let him catch me. That had been different. And he'd always wanted to, I knew. And I wish I'd let him once or twice.

I took Con's shooter out of my jacket pocket and laid it down on the bricks next to me and then I took out my fags and lit up.

It's nearly full light now. From where I am I can see the sweep of the river for a good twelve miles and to my right, inland, the glow of the steelworks is pink against the grey sky.

I scan the yard. There is no sign of Eric. But he's there. Somewhere. And when he moves I'll see him. Even if he scratches his arse.

I smoke my fag and when I've finished it I throw it out over the vat and watch it spiral down until it hits the water and hisses and dies.

When I look up again I see Eric.

He is crawling face down along the top of the low kiln that is covered in grass. He must have been there all the time, waiting and sweating and listening. He'd never thought to look up. He probably thought I was half a mile down the river poking sticks into bushes.

I let him crawl a little further before I speak. This is too nice to rush.

'Eric,' I say.

The sound of my voice bounces off the water in the vat and echoes round its walls.

Eric stops crawling. His head jerks about from side to side, trying to see where my voice is coming from.

'Over here,' I say. 'I'm up here, Eric.'

This time he freezes. When he finally manages to move again his head swivels slowly round until he's looking at me.

The movement is like that of a lizard on a warm rock.

'Get up,' I say.

He gets up. He doesn't take his eyes off my face.

'Down,' I say.

He doesn't move. I show him Con's shooter.

'I said down.'

He walks to the edge of the kiln and slithers down its eroded overgrown side.

'Lean against the kiln. With your back to me.'

He stretches his arms out and does as he's told. There is nothing else he can do.

I climb down from the kiln and stand and look at Eric for a minute or two. Then I ease myself up on to the edge of the vat next to the shotgun and the bottle.

'Turn round,' I say.

He turns round. I look into his face and I smile. Then I unscrew the top of the bottle.

'You look as though you could use a drink,' I say.

He sways slightly and tries to straighten up again but he can't quite make the true vertical again.

'So why don't you join me? After all, you were a drinking mate of my brother. Weren't you?'

A skein of geese flies over from off the river.

'Come here,' I say.

He seems to have difficulty in putting one foot in front of the other. When he finally gets to me I pick up the bottle.

'Let's have this one with Frank,' I say.

He doesn't move.

'Take it,' I say.

Somehow he manages to stretch out an arm and take the bottle. I look into his eyes until he forces himself to lift the bottle to his mouth. He tips the bottle and opens his mouth but because he is trying not to swallow, the whisky runs out of the sides of his mouth and down his neck and chin.

'Swallow it, Eric,' I say. 'Every drop. Just like it was with Frank.'

He puts the bottle to his mouth again and takes a sip and then another and the third time I put my hand to the base of the bottle and hold it tilted so that he's either got to drink or choke.

This is where I am very wrong.

I have one hand on the bottle and my other hand is gripping the inside edge of the vat to stop me falling forward as I tilt the bottle.

I am wide open.

The movement is very slight. I'm concentrating on his face and it isn't until I hear the thin click that those things have that I know what is happening.

For a split second there is unbelievable coolness. The bottle smashes on the edge of the vat. Then the heat comes and the pain climbs inside me.

As the blade leaves me I fall sideways along the edge of the vat. Eric lunges for the shotgun but as I roll over I catch the stock with my foot and the gun slides off the rim and clatters down inside the vat. I continue rolling and for a moment I am staring up into the sky and it is red. Then I fall. I land on my back, my torso on a pile of bricks, my legs in a few inches of water.

Something is sticking up into my field of vision down near my right knee. It is the butt of the shotgun. I stretch my hand out towards it. My fingers are nearly there but the pain is too much and I have to let my arm splash down useless in the shallow water by my side. Then Eric appears, standing on the edge of the vat. I raise my arm and try for the shotgun again. When Eric sees what I am trying to do he jumps down into the vat splashing water up the sides and as my fingers close on the butt he kicks my hand away and drags the shotgun from underneath me causing me to slide off the bricks and end up wholly in the shallow water.

I close my eyes to shut out the pain and when I open them again Eric is standing over me, shouting something but I can't understand the words. Still shouting he lifts the shotgun to his shoulder and draws the hammer back.

Then he stops shouting and takes careful aim at my head. The thought strikes me that there is no need for him to do that. Not at this range.

I watch his fingers as they tighten on the trigger. His hands seem very close. There is a ring with the initial E on it, on the third finger of his right hand.

The gun goes off and the sound of thunder echoes round the vat. The noise explodes into my body. Birds race across the sky.

There is a ringing silence. When I open my eyes Eric is no longer standing over me.

Pain wells up in me again and I look down to my stomach. The blood is pumping out too quickly. Much too quickly. The water round me is becoming streaked with thin red lines that swirl slowly towards my feet.

But surprisingly there is no evidence of the shotgun blast. The blood that is creeping out of me is coming from the knife wound.

I look beyond my feet. Eric is lying on his back at the far end of the vat. All I can really see of him is one leg bent double, the knee pointing up to the sky.

I can't see his face at all because his head is out of sight below the line of his chest. But I don't think there would be very much face for me to see. The water around Eric is much redder than it is around me.

And between us, beyond my feet, half in the water, is the shotgun, what's left of it, twisted and black, still smoking, the smoke curling up into the grey morning sky.

Faint sunlight warms my face. The water's surface ripples for a second as a slight wind drifts in and then out of the vat.

There is the sound of a car. A long way away. The sound stops. A door slams. Time passes and I carry on staring up into the sky.

The pain went a long time ago.

Now I can hear someone moving aimlessly through the foliage near the kiln. Footsteps approach the vat. Suddenly they stop.

I try and call out but no words come. There is a movement at the edge of the vat. Out of the corner of my eye I can see a hand touching the smashed remains of the whisky bottle. I manage to move my arm and a piece

315

of brick makes a small splash in the water by my side. Con's face appears at the rim. For a while he just stares down into the vat.

'Jesus Christ,' he says softly. 'Jesus H. Christ.'

Then he scrambles over the top and drops down next to me, squatting on his haunches. He looks at my wound with interest.

'Well now, Jack,' he says half to himself. 'What's to do. What is to do?'

I stare at his face but I can't speak.

'I'm supposed to take you back to Gerald and Les. Yes, indeed. That's what I'm supposed to do.'

He pushed his hat back on his head.

'But this, I would say, makes things different. That's what I would say.'

He looks at the wound again and thoughts pass through his mind. Suddenly he stands up and brushes his coat down. He turns away from me and has a closer look at Eric. 'Jesus H. Christ,' he says again. Then he notices his shooter lying on the wall where I left it. He picks it up and looks it over. He slips it in his pocket and clambers over the edge of the vat without looking back. I hear him jump down on the other side and begin to walk away. Then there is silence for a long time until I hear the car door slam again and the engine start up and I listen to the sound until it dies away and then there is nothing, nothing at all.

The publishers hope that this book has given you enjoyable reading. Large Print Books are especially designed to be as easy to see and hold as possible. If you wish a complete list of our books please ask at your local library or write directly to:

Dales Large Print Books
Magna House, Long Preston,
Skipton, North Yorkshire.
BD23 4ND

This Large Print Book for the partially sighted, who cannot read normal print, is published under the auspices of

THE ULVERSCROFT FOUNDATION